SURVIVE THE END

A POST-APOCALYPTIC SURVIVAL THRILLER - ATOMIC THREAT BOOK 3

DAVE BOWMAN

Copyright © 2020 by Dave Bowman

All rights reserved.

No part of this book may be reproduced in any form or by any electronic or mechanical means, including information storage and retrieval systems, without written permission from the author, except for the use of brief quotations in a book review.

1

11:34 AM - WHITE ROCK, ARIZONA

There were six guards, and Jack was watching all of them.

From the roof of a three-story building, he could see their hiding places.

They were stationed near the interstate, dotted behind buildings and clusters of trees. They shifted restlessly, waiting for a vehicle to appear on I-10.

Since running vehicles were few and far between, they didn't concern themselves much with staying hidden during this downtime. The sound of a distant engine traveling east or west on the interstate would give them plenty of time to position themselves out of sight from a driver's vantage point.

Then, if a driver stopped to siphon gas from one of the abandoned vehicles clustered in that area, the six guards would ambush them.

And if the driver didn't stop? Jack suspected the men would start shooting at the passing vehicle, trying to kill or wound the driver.

These guys were serious. They meant to steal every car that passed through the small city.

But stealing cars was the least of their crimes. Jack knew that firsthand.

Most of the men sat, yawning and trying to stay awake. A couple of them paced anxiously back and forth. They wiped the sweat from their brows, hot and red from the late morning Arizona sun.

Must be hard work terrorizing an entire city, he thought to himself as he watched the men with disgust.

Jack squinted through the scope of his rifle. He had spent most of the morning searching for ammo. He kept his search confined to the downtown area, where he knew the gang members wouldn't venture. Even hardened criminals had their limits. They didn't want to spend time in the city center where a nuclear bomb had blown a huge swath of the city to smithereens.

Miraculously, he had found some ammunition for his firearm in the manager's office of a greasy spoon diner. The restaurant had stood just beyond the blast radius, and it had survived the explosion. Jack was discovering all kinds of things people had kept behind closed doors, safe from the world to see.

And now, that restaurant manager's foresight would mean that Jack could go back into the gang's territory.

Back into hell. Where they had kept Jack prisoner, handcuffed and chained to a bed for two nights as punishment for back-talking their leader.

Well, not just punishment.

They had intended to break Jack, both physically and mentally. That was how they had taken over this small city. They had broken people's wills, stripped them of any hope of ever escaping and returning to freedom.

But they hadn't succeeded. Not on Jack.

Through luck and sheer will, he managed to escape that blood-soaked motel they had kept him in.

But Naomi and Brent were still being held in those prisons.

Jack had fought so hard to escape, and now he was going back in. But first, he had to get the gatekeepers out of the way.

The sun rose higher. A few minutes later, two of the men rose to their feet. They said something to the other remaining men. Then the first two guards walked away, heading south toward the gang's headquarters.

Just as Jack expected.

Two days before, when he, Naomi, and Brent had been ambushed on this very interstate, it had been around high noon. The men who captured them had taken the trio to their headquarters. There, Jack, Naomi, and Brent had been assessed, split up, and sent to separate detention centers.

And who had been there at the headquarters, seated at a table and stuffing their faces with food cooked by their prisoners?

The core twelve members of the gang. The ones who called the shots and were in charge of this operation.

Below them were countless lower-ranked members. The trusted ones were armed guards. They were stationed at the entrance points to the gang's territory. They watched over the workers, the drones – the prisoners. They made sure the prisoners didn't revolt.

The four men Jack now watched were the mid-level guys. Entrusted with weapons, loyal enough to run the carjacking operation, they were vetted members of the gang. But they weren't the *elite* members.

The two men walking south toward the adobe house

were part of the elite crew – the core twelve members. And it was lunchtime.

In his short interactions with these guys, Jack had watched them closely. The twelve men at the top were too power-drunk to give up their special privileges like a daily feast with their buddies. Not even after the crisis situation of last night. Not even when their numbers had been reduced by two.

At least Jack *thought* two of the core members had been killed last night.

Oscar, the leader of the group, had been the one to assess new prisoners. He'd raked his eyes over Jack, Naomi, and Brent as they stood in that big adobe house two days ago and decided which detention center – prison – to send them. He'd been calling the shots.

But then last night, Dox, the second in command, had burst into Jack's room and announced he was taking things over. Dox had killed the leader.

And then Jack had killed Dox, just before making his escape.

Now, just ten of the leaders were left standing. And they were all meeting in the headquarters right now. In just a few minutes, they'd be stuffed and sleepy, leaning back in their chairs and unbuckling their belts as Jack had seen them do two days ago.

Now, Jack watched the two guards abandon their posts and disappear over the hill, headed toward that big adobe house where they ran their operation.

And Jack happened to know that adobe bricks had excellent sound insulation properties. The guys meeting in that fancy house might not hear gunshots some distance away on the interstate.

Down below, the remaining four guards ate packed lunches of sandwiches and packaged food.

Good.

The guard Jack would have to worry about the most was the closest one. The tall, wiry man stood behind a nearby building. He hadn't sat down once. He paced back and forth, full of nervous energy. He scanned the area constantly. Jack had to be careful not to give his own position away.

Jack's eyes darted to the stand of junipers along the edge of the highway, where he monitored two more guards. One was lazy and half-asleep, but the other was on high alert, clutching his rifle and studying the area.

The fourth was farther away, on the far side of the interstate, stationed behind an abandoned car beside the meridian.

Four guards. And not only would Jack have to get rid of them, but he'd also have to go down there and take a couple of their weapons. The magazines he'd found were of some help for his cause, but they weren't enough. Not for what was coming after this initial confrontation.

And the only protection he had was a flimsy wooden outcropping at the edge of the roof. It covered him fairly well. His enemies wouldn't be able to see him clearly. But the outcropping didn't offer much physical protection. Bullets would easily pierce the flimsy wooden structure. If he was going to survive this, he would have to keep down.

The guard nearest him would have the best view of Jack's position. Jack planned to take him out first. Jack watched him now, pacing back and forth and munching on potato chips.

It was almost time for Jack to make his move.

The guards were distracted with their lunch. It would be

easier now. Jack would have to keep this short – dispose of them, then use the access ladder on the back of the building to get to the ground level as quickly as possible. He would pick up the weapons from the closest guard, then he would clear the area.

Though the ten core members were blocks away, enjoying their lunch in the adobe house, the sound of gunfire would alert other, closer members of the group. No doubt there were several other checkpoints along the interstate. The sound of Jack's rifle – and the blasts from the guards as they would return fire – would send dozens more men running.

Jack would have to get out of sight before they arrived.

As soon as the first round fired, time would start ticking. He'd have only moments to finish the whole thing.

Over in the juniper trees, the lazy guard was chowing down on a sandwich. Even the guard on high alert had shouldered his rifle while he drained the last of his soda. On the far side of the interstate, the guard behind the car gave a quick look around before he began picking the lettuce off his sandwich.

Everything was riding on this moment. Somewhere in the gang's territory, locked away in one of their makeshift work camps, Naomi and Brent were being kept prisoner. They were being forced to work. All of their hopes of making it to safety in Texas were becoming distant memories. They needed him.

And somewhere in central Texas, Jack's wife needed him too. Perhaps she was struggling at that very moment, hoping against hope that her husband would make it home to her alive.

There was no room for mistakes.

Jack took a deep breath. He sighted the closest guard. Just as the guard made it to the end of his pacing loop, he turned and started moving away from Jack.

Jack steadied himself. His trigger finger began to tense. Then, sure of his target, he pulled the trigger.

The shot rang out through the sleepy, quiet town, its noise echoing between the buildings lining the interstate.

The guard stumbled forward a few steps, then fell to the concrete like a felled tree.

Jack focused on him a split second more, just enough time to send another round into the guy's back.

Keeping himself low, Jack swiveled the barrel toward the men in the junipers.

The standing guard had dropped his soda bottle and swung his rifle up to aim. He began to open fire on Jack. His aim was low. Jack used the opportunity to return fire.

Soon, the guard dropped his gun and fell to his side.

Two down.

The farthest guard began shooting as well. But his aim was way off. Jack stayed where he was and focused on the next target.

The slower guy in the trees had finally lifted his rifle. But before he could open fire, Jack hit him. The man lay sprawled on his back, immobile.

Jack turned his sight toward the man by the meridian. He shot off a few rounds, but his aim was off by several feet to the right. He hadn't adjusted for the effects of the wind across such a large distance.

Meanwhile, the guard's aim was getting better. Bullets whizzed by Jack's head, and Jack ducked down for a moment. Keeping below the outcropping, he inched over toward the side.

Then, he raised his rifle again. Doing his best to correct for the discrepancy in elevation and the wind, he adjusted his aim. He fired several shots toward the man, who had continued aiming at Jack's original position.

Finally, the guy yelled in agony. Jack fired off another round or two. Soon the guard was down, splayed out on the pavement below.

Jack took a breath. The first part was over.

Now, he would just need a quick look at the surroundings before heading to the ladder.

The two men in the trees were dead.

The first guard –

Jack swallowed.

The first guard was gone. He was still alive, as Jack could tell from the trail of blood leading away from the sidewalk. And the guard had taken his rifle with him.

Panicked, Jack scanned the area below. He pushed himself to his feet, ran to the opposite wall and looked at the area below.

Nothing. No sign of the first guard.

Jack had lost him. And any second now, more men would show up. Jack looked around frantically.

He had to get off the roof.

He ran toward the access ladder at full sprint. Once there, he dropped down to a crouch. Kneeling behind the wooden roof outcropping, he waited a moment.

He heard nothing, no movement or sound, save the pounding of his own heart.

Behind him, voices shouted from farther west on the interstate.

They were coming for him.

He dared to raise his head just a bit, just enough to see over the edge through his scope.

There was a flash of movement behind a garbage dumpster.

Jack aimed. But he was too late.

Off to the side, behind a parked car, another shooter that Jack hadn't spotted opened fire.

All at once, he was trapped.

The two shooters unleashed an onslaught of bullets toward the roof, sending bits of wood from the outcropping flying in every direction.

Jack flattened himself to the ground. The rounds were coming too fast. He was unable to return fire.

2

SUNDAY, 6:22 A.M. - THE TEXAS HILL COUNTRY

Annie woke up shivering.

She looked over at Harvey. He was still asleep. Or unconscious, rather. Charlotte was sleeping in the passenger seat of the car.

Annie grabbed the pistol from her side and stood up awkwardly. Her muscles were tight from having spent the night sitting upright on the ground.

She had dozed off for a bit. She guessed she hadn't been asleep for long. The sun still hadn't risen, and she had already spent long hours keeping watch through the night.

She had managed to stay awake for most of the night, sitting in the grass and propped up against the car. Though Harvey was still tied up, he was dangerous. She had made the knots on his wrists and ankles tight, but she didn't trust the rope completely. Not after he had shot Charlotte.

She rubbed her hands over her arms, trying to warm her skin. The temperature had fallen overnight, and dew had collected on the weeds. The dampness of the early morning chilled her to the core.

Though she had been tempted to spend the night inside

the shelter and relative warmth of the car, it would have been too risky. If Harvey had woken up, he might have gotten free of his bindings. He had already tried to steal their Porsche. He had snatched the .22 out of Charlotte's hands and turned it against her. And then the worst had happened.

He had shot Charlotte.

Somehow, Annie had managed to stop the bleeding, but just barely.

Harvey would regain consciousness with a splitting headache, only to find himself tied up. He would be furious.

Annie shivered again. This time, she wasn't sure if it was the cold or the fear of another confrontation that made her pull the sweater tighter around her neck.

Still though, she hadn't shot him. And she had her reasons. Their car was hopelessly stuck in a muddy ditch. And he had mentioned something about a farm nearby. Maybe if he had a gun pointed at him – by someone *competent* with firearms this time – he would be willing to help them push the car out of the ditch. Maybe there was some equipment on the farm that could help them. Or maybe there were more people that could help push the Porsche out.

But he was still out cold. Annie thought he would have woken up by now. She knew she had given him a good crack on the head with a glass bottle, but she hadn't expected him to stay out this long.

She's squinted over at his dark shape in the grass nearby. Was he dead?

She inched over toward him, careful not to rustle the grass too much. It was still dark, so she had to get close to him to get a good look. *Too* close for her taste. She felt her heart quicken as she bent down to look at him. She gripped the pistol, her palms growing sweaty despite the cold.

He was still alive. His chest was rising and falling like clockwork.

Annie moved away from him again. She bent to pick up Harvey's cowboy hat from where she had left it in the grass. Feeling the stiffness in her back, she straightened up and perched the hat on her red hair. It provided at least a little warmth.

She would have to make a decision. Spend another day stuck in the car, hoping that someone would magically appear to help push them out of the ditch? Wait for Harvey to come to, then force him to help? Or try to walk the countless miles to safety at Jack's old house in the country?

She didn't like any of those options. Annie couldn't count on anyone to help them anymore. Not since the EMP and nuclear attacks had made everyone just about go crazy. The EMP – the electromagnetic pulse that had destroyed the electrical grid and rendered most vehicles useless – had started the mass panic, and the nuclear attack had sealed the deal. They were living in social collapse, and it wasn't pretty.

No one could be trusted, especially not the lying attempted murderer drooling on himself in the grass. And besides, Annie doubted Charlotte could walk very far with her injury. Certainly not over a hundred miles to Jack's family house.

It would be up to Annie to figure out how to get them home.

She moved toward the car and opened the passenger door, kneeling at Charlotte's side. Her friend frowned, then slowly opened her heavy eyes.

Charlotte blinked at her a moment, confused at first.

Then everything sunk in all at once, especially the pain. She screwed her face up.

"Ow," she murmured as she shifted in her seat.

Annie checked her wounds. There had been some seepage overnight. She grabbed her supplies – she'd have to change the bandages. But first, they'd have to do something for the pain.

It seemed to Annie that there was an art to pain management. If they stayed on top of Charlotte's pain, making sure it didn't get too out of control, they could manage it. But if they let the pain go too long, it was harder to bring it back down. Charlotte had already waken up three times in agony. The biggest problem was that the only painkillers they had were ibuprofen and vodka.

"Another swig?" Annie asked, reaching for the bottle of the alcohol.

"Sure," Charlotte said, grimacing. "Hair of the dog and all. I'm practically hungover from yesterday."

Annie helped her take a drink, then capped the bottle. Annie used some of their limited water supply to wash her own hands, then began changing Charlotte's dressings.

"Is the cowboy still unconscious?" Charlotte asked, flinching as Annie removed the gauze over the entrance wound.

"Yep," Annie said. "Out like a light."

"Good. But I still think we should shoot him."

"We may have to," Annie said, glancing over at him. She took a deep breath. "Listen, I'm thinking about going to check out that farm he was talking about."

Charlotte looked at her. "What, now? You can't leave me alone here!"

"I won't be gone for long. And I'll leave the pistol with

you," Annie said. "If he wakes up and gives you any trouble, just shoot him."

Charlotte scoffed. "We both know how well that went the last time."

"Yeah, but now you'll be ready. Last time you hesitated. Now you're mad. I don't doubt that you have it in you to pull the trigger this time."

"Well, that's for sure," Charlotte said bitterly. "But why do you want to go on a wild goose chase after some imaginary farm, anyway? Harvey was probably lying about having a family farm down the road. He lied about everything else."

"True, but there's bound to be some kind of homestead around here," Annie said, frowning as she cut a new length of gauze from the roll. "Maybe they have some equipment that would help us. Or a couple of people to help push."

Charlotte laughed skeptically. "Or to shoot us both."

"I know it's risky, but I don't have a lot of options," Annie said. "You can't walk, can you?"

Charlotte shot her a look.

"I didn't think so," Annie said. "And we can't stay here for a week while you recover. We don't have enough water or food. And what if another guy like Harvey shows up?"

Charlotte chewed on her lip. She sighed. "I guess you're right. You're always right."

Charlotte glanced at the pistol, and Annie knew she was thinking of their run-in with the psychopath, Dan, the other day. Annie had never wanted to get in Dan's car. She had never trusted him. And in the end, her instincts had been correct.

"Just be careful, okay?" Charlotte pleaded. "And don't stay gone too long."

"I won't. And you'll have to stay awake while I'm gone. I

need you to be alert in case he wakes up. Do you think you can do that?"

"Knowing that I'm alone with him," Charlotte jerked her head toward Harvey, "I couldn't sleep if I tried."

Annie nodded, then moved on to the exit wound on Charlotte's back. Charlotte groaned in pain as she bent forward.

Annie bit her lip, careful not to gasp at the gruesome sight and scare Charlotte. The second wound looked about as bad as the first. They didn't look infected, but they didn't look too great, either. Annie didn't want Charlotte to know, but they didn't have enough first aid supplies to stay there another day. They would soon run out of gauze and medical tape. And Annie didn't know what she'd do for her friend without those essentials.

Annie concentrated as she worked, trying to use the least amount of gauze possible to get the job done. Finally, she was finished. She brought Charlotte's shirt down and put her supplies away. She handed Charlotte one of her pills to treat her Addison's disease, then pushed herself to her feet.

Orange light was beginning to appear on the eastern horizon. Soon, the sun would be up.

"Do you need anything before I go?" Annie asked, dusting herself off.

"Can I have another granola bar?"

Annie smiled and grabbed her one from the back. "Here," she said. "And don't forget this."

Carefully, Annie handed Charlotte the .22. Charlotte took the gun and placed it gingerly in her lap.

"You remember about the safety?" Annie asked.

"Yeah, yeah," Charlotte said dismissively. She squinted

down at the gun. "The safety is on now. I have to turn it off before I can shoot."

"Good," Annie said. She stood with her hands on her hips, surveying the scene. She grabbed a granola bar and tore into it.

"Go on," Charlotte said, meeting Annie's eyes and smiling wryly. "Let's get this over with."

Annie smiled, gave a quick nod, then spun on her feet. "I'll be back soon," she called over her shoulder.

Annie set out toward the west. Though nervous about leaving Charlotte alone, she was excited to cover new ground, to get away from the desolate strip of road they had been stuck on for a day and a half. Other than the semi-truck sprawled across the two-lane highway nearby, the surrounding area was empty. They hadn't seen any houses for several miles before she'd lost control of the Porsche and swerved off the road. Annie hoped there would be a house nearby to the west.

Walking briskly, she covered the distance quickly. As she scaled a steep hill, she looked back at the Porsche one last time. On the other side of the hill, it was out of sight. Stretching ahead of her were pastures and fields, green from the rains the week before. It was mostly wild land in this part of the Texas Hill Country, mixed in with cattle ranches and farm fields. To her right were some limestone cliffs dotted with cedars. To her left was a fenced-off expanse of partially forested land. No farms in sight, at least not yet.

With the sun nearly at the horizon behind her, the sky was brightening, and the features of the land were starting to take shape. This was comforting to Annie, and she felt her shoulders loosen up a bit. She hated leaving Charlotte alone with Harvey. But she had faith that Charlotte could defend herself if necessary.

What worried her most of all was facing whatever might be waiting for her out in this wild country. And she was unarmed. If only they had two guns!

If only Jack's gun hadn't been stolen.

But that was behind her. She couldn't waste the mental energy regretting the squatters now occupying her own home back in Austin. She had to keep looking forward. She had to figure out a plan for them. That was the only way they were going to survive.

She felt herself break into an easy jog. She hadn't realized how cooped up she had felt the past few days. First, hiding out in Dan's house, then keeping vigil at Charlotte's side. Annie had felt a bit stir-crazy with all that sitting around. Now it felt good to be moving, her lungs and her legs working hard. She ran faster, pushing herself to go up and down the hills one after another. The faster she ran, the sooner she would find a solution to her impossible predicament.

Annie scaled yet another rolling hill, then came to a stop at the crest of the rise.

There was a house down there.

Off to the right, a large field was cleared and surrounded by a tall fence along its perimeter. At the far edge of the field, at the end of a long dirt driveway, stood a single-story wooden farmhouse. A few outbuildings were scattered nearby – a barn, maybe, and a shed or two. It was hard to make it all out in the dim light, and Annie couldn't see whether it was occupied or in what kind of shape the property was in. But it was something. And the first man-made structure on the road in miles.

As she caught her breath, a smile spread across her face. Finally, a glimmer of hope.

Annie jogged down the hill, reaching the bottom

quickly. She followed the road as it curved to the right, leading her to the beginning of the long driveway.

Annie slowed to a stop and looked around. An empty field stretched out to the west. It looked like cattle had been kept on the land at one point, but not recently. It stood empty and unused, and weeds grew tall. Seeing that no one was working the land made her hesitate. What if the place was empty? Maybe it had been abandoned long ago. Maybe she'd make better use of her time by looking for another house farther to the west.

After a moment, she shrugged and started up the driveway. If it was empty, it wouldn't be that much of a loss. And a few steps down the driveway, she got a better view of the property. The house looked to be in decent repair. And even better, a newer truck sat parked off to the side behind some oak trees. The truck was too new and valuable to have been left on an abandoned property. Someone was living there.

"Hello!" Annie called out with her hands cupped around her mouth. "Anyone home?"

She waited and listened.

"Hello?" she called louder. "Hel-looo?"

She slowed her pace as she got closer to the house. She didn't want to startle anyone. That alone could cause her to be shot, especially with everyone's nerves on edge after the attacks.

Finally, she came to a stop at the edge of the front yard.

"Is anyone here?" she called toward the house. "I was hoping somebody could help me. My car is stuck in a ditch down the road. And my friend is hurt –"

Annie stopped herself. She felt silly talking to the house. Maybe no one was home. The whole thing had probably been a waste of time. But she figured she might as well knock on the door. Surely if anyone were home, they would've heard her shouting by now. But, just in case, she crossed the yard and began to climb the steps to the front porch.

"Hello, hello? Anyone home?" She shouted in the direction of the window.

On the second step, an overwhelming odor assaulted her senses. It was putrid and intense. Instantly, she realized it was the smell of death – of rotting bodies.

Suddenly, her heart was in her throat. Her eyes fell on the window near the front door. Inside the house, she saw someone sitting in an armchair. All at once, her throat went dry. She wanted to run, but for a split second, her legs felt heavy as lead.

The person in the armchair was dead.

It was an elderly man, and his body slumped over the side of the recliner. His discolored arm dangled over the edge of the armrest.

Annie jolted herself out of her momentary freeze. She stumbled backwards down the steps, then turned and began to run across the yard.

Behind her, something was happening. A noise. A movement – coming from inside the house.

Terror filled Annie to her core. She ran through the tall grass of the yard. And to her horror, she heard the front door swing open behind her.

Annie propelled herself forward, picking up speed as she reached the driveway.

But someone was on her tail. Footsteps pounded on the porch, then moved across the yard. He was gaining on her.

She glanced quickly over her shoulder as she turned toward the road. She caught only a glimpse of the young man running after her – his dilated, crazed eyes, his pasty skin. She had time for only fragmented thoughts. Had he killed the old man inside? Was she going to be next?

She heard him breathing right behind her, getting closer. She caught only a glimpse of the young man as he closed the distance – his arms reaching out, the gray of his sweatshirt as he moved.

Then he tackled her. He grabbed her around her shoulders and pulled. She tried to tear away from him, but he was too fast.

Annie felt the wind knocked out of her. In one dizzying movement, she slammed against the driveway, hitting the gravel hard.

3

SUNDAY, 7:02 A.M. - WHITE ROCK, ARIZONA

"Rise and shine, sweetheart."

Brent squinted at the harsh light shining in his eyes. He turned over in his bed to see one of the guards standing in the doorway, shining a flashlight on the thin, bare mattress where Brent lay. As always, the guard was carrying a semi-automatic rifle.

"Out of bed. *Now,* 155," the man barked at him.

Brent swung his legs around to the floor and felt the cold, dirty tiles under his feet. The man with the gun took a step inside the room, and plunked a tray of food on the bed beside Brent.

"Eat up," the guard said, grinning. "You'll need your energy today."

He turned and left, locking the door behind him.

Brent lightly rubbed his aching side, which was still painful from two days ago. Then he looked down at the tray of food the guard had left on the mattress. There was the same gray stew he got every meal – full of reconstituted potatoes and some kind of fake meat substance. In the compartment next to it, a small package of crackers. An off-brand juice pack stood at the far corner of the tray, completing the meal.

Brent took the plastic spoon allotted him, and began to choke the food down. He was hungry. Ignoring the nausea provoked by the colorless food, he ate it quickly. It was dark in the room, and he didn't want any cockroaches crawling in his food like last time when he didn't eat it quickly enough.

He had spent two nights in that disgusting room. How many more would there be? These people – whoever they were – seemed to have no intention of letting him or the other prisoners go anytime soon.

He was quickly finished with the paltry meal and drink. Leaning against the wall, he ran his fingers along his jaw. It was swollen and bruised. Sighing, he reached under the bed, groping in the dark for his eyeglasses. The frames had been twisted and the lenses scratched badly, but at least they weren't destroyed.

Yesterday, when the prisoners were being marched to the work site, Brent had seen a prisoner falling over fire hydrants and walking into trees. The prisoner had complained that he couldn't see anything without his glasses. In response, the guard had given him a swift kick in his back.

Brent waited for the guard who'd brought breakfast to return to the room. It wouldn't be long. Outside, the sun was probably rising, and daylight was wasting. These guys wanted to get as much work out of the prisoners as possible.

He was on the fourth floor of a college dormitory. At first, on that horrible day he'd been captured, they had taken him to the first floor. But then, after the *incident*, they had moved Brent up to this room. Plywood was nailed over all the windows. And without power, candles, or flashlights,

Brent and the other prisoners were in total darkness in their rooms.

As far as Brent could tell, all prisoners on the fourth floor were locked up in a room by themselves – solitary confinement. The first floor had been different. On the first floor, he'd had a roommate. But that hadn't lasted for long.

The door flew open, and the guard returned. This time, a second armed guard stood in the doorway while the first approached Brent.

"On your feet, 155!" the first guard ordered.

Brent stood up, facing the wall, and waited while the man handcuffed him. On the first floor, some of the guys got plastic zip ties around their hands. Up here, it was metal cuffs for everyone.

"March!" the guard ordered.

Brent walked out the hall and followed the ten or twelve other prisoners already heading down the stairs. Armed guards watched them closely and followed them down the stairs to the first floor. None of the prisoners spoke. Everyone with half a brain had learned that talking to other prisoners would result in a beating.

On the ground level, Brent waited off to the side as the guards assigned the prisoners work duty. They were split off into small groups. Each high-risk prisoner like Brent was grouped with four or five low-risk prisoners. Once the men were all arranged into small groups, the guards led them to their work sites. Brent followed the guard and the rest of his group outside the dorm building.

Brent felt a wave of relief each time he was allowed outside. The building he was detained in was claustrophobic and disgusting. And there was always the worry that the guards would somehow forget about him. After all, this wasn't a *real* prison. This whole thing was just a slapped-together operation by some wannabe gangsters and their supporters. These guys didn't know what they were doing.

Outside, he felt he could breathe again. He knew he'd have to do back-breaking work, but at least he wasn't locked up in that dark little room.

The guards led the men to a makeshift latrine – really, just a hole in the ground with some sawdust to scatter on top. The guard uncuffed each prisoner one at a time and gave him a few moments to relieve himself. Their only privacy were some scattered bushes. Depriving the prisoners of human dignity was part of the process, it seemed to Brent. Everything was designed to break them down psychologically.

Once the prisoners were finished, the guards led the men down the street to the north one block, then west a few blocks. They passed other men working. Some were hauling materials, some were digging latrines. Down one street, some teenagers on bicycles pulled small trailers loaded down with packages of food – supervised by guards on bikes, of course. All of them worked in total silence.

Brent looked carefully at each of the groups. He never saw Jack.

And he never saw any women. There had been no trace of Naomi or Jack since they had been separated two days ago.

The women prisoners were kept completely separate from the men. Brent saw a couple of female guards now and then, but no female inmates. Naomi and the other women must have been kept in a separate part of town.

Finally, the guards stopped the group of men in front of an abandoned lot. Brent and the other men looked at each other wordlessly. What work job were they to perform today, they all wondered?

Nearby, a couple of young guys were unloading their bicycle-pulled trailers. They put their tools on the ground, then rode off on their bikes. Once they were gone, Brent's crew was led to the end of the block, where the teens had dumped off some supplies. Brent got a look at what they had left behind: shovels.

"You're first, 155," the guard Brent knew best said, looking in Brent's direction. The guard had a huge tattoo of a spider's web across his neck. The other guards called him Spider.

Spider picked up a shovel and led Brent toward the far corner of the empty lot. The weeds were tall, and the lot was littered with garbage and debris. Once Spider was satisfied with their location, he stopped. He unlocked Brent's handcuffs, handed him the shovel, then raised his rifle threateningly.

"Don't even think about trying anything, 155," Spider warned, narrowing his beady eyes at Brent. "Start digging."

Brent stabbed the shovel in the ground. The earth was dry and hard. The digging wouldn't be easy. He jumped on the top edges of the shovel, driving it into the ground. Then, lifting a shovelful of dry, rocky soil, he tossed the dirt behind him.

"That's the spirit, 155," Spider said between guffaws. "Guess you got the hang of it yesterday."

Brent didn't look up at him as he drove the shovel into the ground again. He snuck a glance at the other men, who were stationed at scattered points around the empty lot. The other five prisoners were guarded by only two men. Brent was assigned his own guard because he was what they considered a flight risk.

Brent sighed, breathing out a mixture of exasperation and dread.

If only he had been more alert back on the highway. If only he had been paying more attention when Jack was siphoning the gas for the Pathfinder two days ago, he wouldn't be doing slave labor for these lunatics.

The thing was, Brent *had* been alert out there on the interstate. And he was pretty sure Naomi had been paying attention, too. Those guys had attacked them out of nowhere. They must have have been waiting in damned good hiding places for who knows how long when Jack had stopped the Pathfinder for gas. There had been no movement, no noise, no sight of the men as they lay in wait. Out of nowhere, the guards had attacked Brent and his friends, surrounding them and pointing rifles at them.

Brent, Jack, and Naomi never even had a chance.

And now, the three of them were prisoners.

The people who had ambushed Brent's group had led them to a big adobe house – their headquarters. There, the leaders of this operation had assigned Brent, Jack, and Naomi to separate detention facilities. Camps, they had called them. But really, they were prisons.

Jack, Naomi, and Brent had been handcuffed, then led away by armed guards. Though Brent had tried to see where his friends had been taken, the guards made sure that his friends' whereabouts were kept a mystery.

Jack had been led in the opposite direction from the others – back toward the interstate. Jack had mouthed off to the head honcho, Oscar. And Oscar had sent him to the C Block. Brent assumed it was a facility for the worst offenders. He shuddered to think what they were doing to Jack now.

And Brent hadn't seen where Naomi had been taken, either. Brent's guards had led him away from the main road. They'd taken him to the west several blocks, then to the

Survive the End

south. They had taken several turns, probably intentionally to disorient Brent and make him forget his whereabouts.

Brent hadn't seen where Naomi was taken. There had been two men guarding her, but when they got outside, Brent saw that Naomi had been passed off to two female guards. That, at least, was a small sign of hope that maybe Naomi wouldn't be treated too terribly. But still, he worried about her. She had been in such a state of grief before they had been captured. How was she responding now to this horrific turn of events?

That first day, Brent had been taken to the first floor of the dormitory. He had been assigned a room with a middle-aged man named Quinn. That first day had been terrible. Brent was furious, pacing back and forth across the room they had locked him up in, trying to get free of the cuffs. But Quinn was in a panic.

"We have to get out of here!" Quinn had cried. "They're going to kill us! I know they are, I know it!"

Brent had collapsed on his bed in frustration. At that point, his hands had still been cuffed behind him, and Quinn's were too. Brent looked at his roommate. The normally pale, round man had turned red. His nostrils flared as he breathed in and out furiously. He looked over at Brent, suddenly remembering his presence.

"You've got to calm down," Brent said. "You're going to hyperventilate and pass out. Then you'll never get out of here."

Quinn looked at him. "But we've got to escape! You're just lying there! You're not just going to give up, are you?"

"No, I'm not giving up. But I don't know how we can get out of here at the moment," Brent said angrily.

Quinn stared at Brent as if he were unable to believe the younger man's words. Then, all of a sudden, he threw himself at the window. He tried to wedge his shoulder behind the plywood on the window and pry it off, but the panel wouldn't budge. Quinn only succeeded in ripping his shirt and cutting a gash in his shoulder. Next, in a frenzy, Quinn fell on the floor and started to kick the plywood.

Brent closed his eyes, trying to shut out the noise of Quinn's frenzied attempt to escape. Brent was fighting back his own panic, and seeing his roommate go berserk wasn't helping. He began to feel like a weight was pressing against his chest. He found it hard to breathe.

How was he going to get out of this room?

Finally, Quinn collapsed on the floor, groaning and spent from his effort. The plywood hadn't budged.

He looked up at Brent, anguished. "What are we going to do?" Quinn asked. "We've gotta find a way out. Now!"

"I want to get out of here just as much as you do. But we have to think about this. We have to plan our best course of action."

Quinn thought about it for a moment while he caught his breath. "Okay, our plan is to rush them when they open the door."

Brent sighed. "I don't think that's such a good idea. They all have guns. And there are so many of them."

"So, what then?" Quinn demanded angrily. "You're just going to do what they say? Play nice with these . . . these monsters?"

"I don't know," Brent said. "Maybe that's what we'll have to do, at least in the beginning. Maybe we can escape later."

Quinn didn't answer. He just lay on the floor, his face turning redder and redder.

About an hour later, they heard movement in the hall. Brent and Quinn looked at each other. When they heard a key in the door, Quinn scrambled to his feet.

"I'm getting out of here," Quinn muttered under his breath, "with or without you."

"No, wait," Brent said as the doorknob turned and the door began to open. "Wait!"

But Quinn was already charging ahead. Brent rose to his feet, trying to block Quinn. The older man plowed into Brent, pushing the younger man forward just as the door swung open.

"Stop!" Brent yelled.

Then, a deafening blast shot through the room. An incredible force slammed Brent to the floor. He became aware of the feeling of warm, thick liquid on his skin.

At first, Brent thought he had been shot. His looked over his own body, checking for a bullet wound.

Then, he understood what had happened.

The guard had shot Quinn, whose body had fallen on Brent's legs. Brent moved to push Quinn off him, but a force to his side came out of nowhere. Pain seared through his body.

Brent looked up to see the guard lifting the butt of his rifle in the air.

"No one gets out of here!" the guard roared. "There's no escape!"

The rifle slammed into Brent's side again, sending fiery currents through his body. He screamed in agony.

The guard stood over him a moment, watching him. Finally, he gave Brent a push with his steel-toed boot.

"That'll teach you to try to escape," he said. He walked out of the room, leaving Brent lying on the floor.

Brent groaned. Quinn was still lying on top of his legs, pinning Brent in place.

Brent lifted his head up to get a look at the guy. He

shook his legs a little, seeing if Quinn responded to the movement.

He was dead.

Suddenly disgusted by the dead body lying on top of him, Brent struggled to be free of the weight. He pushed the body off him, then squirmed away from him on the floor.

Brent was covered in Quinn's blood.

Brent felt a wave of nausea. He was overcome with an urge to escape from the room, to breathe fresh air.

He looked over at the door. Surprisingly, the guard had left it open. Was this a test? Were they waiting to see if Brent tried to escape?

But a moment later, the guard was back. And this time, he had company. Another man, this one with a shotgun, stood at his back.

"On your feet, 155."

Brent struggled to push himself up. It was hard enough with his hands cuffed behind his back. But now, after the beating he had endured, the pain made it difficult to move. The guards laughed openly as Brent struggled and fumbled.

The guard with the shotgun gave Brent a push out the doorway. "There's been a change of plans. Your new home is the fourth floor."

"But I wasn't trying to escape!" Brent protested. "I was trying to stop the other guy from running out."

The guard brought the butt of his rifle up again. This time, it struck Brent's jaw.

Brent stumbled backward, suddenly dizzy.

He ran his tongue over his teeth. They were all still there. The guard hadn't hit him hard enough to break anything. Brent guessed that meant he was lucky.

"I don't like the sound of your voice, 155," the guard said. He grabbed hold of Brent's collar and tightened it around

Brent's neck. "Keep that big mouth of yours shut, understand?"

He let go of Brent's shirt and gave him a push backward.

And that was how Brent got reassigned to the fourth floor.

They had led him up there, locking him in for solitary confinement. And he had only been let out the following day, when it was time for him to work. Yesterday, the work had been digging a latrine – a long ditch. But today they weren't digging a ditch. The prisoners were scattered around the empty lot. They were digging a massive hole.

Brent dug at his patch of earth slowly but steadily. Yesterday, he had learned that when he stopped to rest, he would get hit. His body still ached from the beating two days ago. He didn't want to be hit again. If he could keep an even, steady pace, he could last until the short water break they gave them every hour, then the lunch break around noon, when unarmed men would bring them trays of that same gray stew.

He was trapped in a nightmarish reality. And there didn't seem to be any way to escape. At least not yet. Brent kept his head down and did the labor they assigned him, but he waited for the moment he'd have a chance to break free. He didn't know when it would come, or how – he was under lock and key, or under the close watch of an armed man, at all times. But he had to keep hope that the chance to escape would come at some point.

If he were to ever lose that hope, he'd just let them shoot him.

And some of the guys – either willingly or not – chose that route. Especially on the first day, Brent had heard several confrontations between prisoners and guards. It always ended with the prisoner being shot dead. Brent suspected that Quinn knew he'd be killed, but chose to go die, anyway. The men who remained knew they'd have to cooperate if they wanted to live.

Brent would have to be alert for any opening, any chance to get out of there. Then he'd have to find Naomi and Jack. As he dug at the rocky earth, that seemed about as likely as going to the moon.

"That's deep enough," Spider grunted. "Start widening it out now."

Brent nodded, then paused just for a second to wipe the sweat from his brow. There was something going on at the far side of the lot. A crew of young guys on bikes had arrived, and some of the older prisoners were unloading their cargo from the bike trailers. Brent squinted in the sun, trying to make sense of the scene. Then, he recoiled in disgust when he realized what the cargo was.

They were unloading dead bodies.

"This ain't break time, 155!" Spider barked. "Get back to digging."

Brent realized with a jolt he had stopped working for too long. The sight of the bodies had shocked him, and he had stood there motionless. Before Spider decided to hit him, Brent got to work with the shovel again.

They were burying the prisoners these guards – these monsters – had shot.

Brent was helping to dig a mass grave.

I have to find a way out of here, he thought as he tossed another shovelful of dirt out of the hole.

I have to get out of here or someone's going to be dumping my body here in a few days.

4

SUNDAY, 10:48 A.M. - NORTHEASTERN, TENNESSEE

The sound of pots clanging to the floor woke Brody Walsh with a start.

Brody opened his eyes to see his mother in the kitchen. She looked over at him guiltily.

Brody shuffled on the couch. The flu-like ache in his limbs reminded him of the events of the past few days all at once.

"Sorry, Brody," she said, picking up a saucepan from the floor. "That was an accident. I was trying to be quiet."

Myra walked over and stopped in front of his place on the couch. "I wanted you to sleep as long as you could. But I needed to do something with that chicken soup I started last night. Don't want it to go bad." She turned and looked out the window in the living room. "It's got to be at least 10:00 or 11:00 in the morning by now."

"It's okay, Mom," Brody said as he stiffly pushed himself up to sit on the couch. "Is Katie still asleep?"

"Last I checked she was," Myra said. "How are you feeling?"

Brody yawned and looked himself over. "Still feel like

death warmed over, but not quite as bad as yesterday, surprisingly. That long sleep must have done me some good."

Myra sat down beside him and put her arm around his shoulders, drawing him close. "I'm just so worried about you! I wish... I wish there was something I could do." She shook her said head sadly. "Radiation poisoning! I just can't believe this is happening!"

Brody sighed. "Yeah, if only I had stayed home. I should have never gone out looking for Kevin. I should've stayed with Katie. Then I wouldn't have gotten sick!"

Myra looked at him. "But it was a good thing to do, all the same. You were just looking out for that little boy. That's how I raised you kids – to care for people."

Brody scoffed. "And look where it got me."

He had already told her everything the night before – how he had searched for the neglected little boy, and how he had been delayed getting home after the nuclear bomb. And the strange symptoms that had showed up the next morning after the radiation exposure.

His words had been hard for Myra to hear. Just like his daughter Katie, Brody's mother had kept insisting that Brody was wrong – maybe he only had the flu. But eventually, his mom had come to understand that it wasn't the flu. She had believed him, but she still searched for some kind of solution. Or some kind of alternate reality in which her son wasn't deathly ill.

Myra clenched her hands in frustration. "But there's got to be something we can do! Some kind of remedy. We could induce vomiting – or you could take some charcoal tablets. That's what they do for poisoning sometimes."

Brody shook his head. "It won't work. Those things are for poisons taken by mouth. This radioactive stuff – I guess it gets to you through your skin. And I already washed off the first day as best I could. The damage has already been done. The fallout – the radiation – whatever it is . . . It's probably made its way to my organs by now."

Myra twisted her hands in worry. "Oh, dear. I – I'm so sorry, Brody." She looked at her son with tears in her eyes. "This can't be happening! I can't lose you. I can't lose my son!"

Brody took her hands in his. "I'm sorry, Mom. It's not fair. None of this is."

The two sat there without speaking for a while. Myra wept quietly, and Brody tried to comfort her. But what could he do? He was slowly being poisoned. And to make matters worse, there was still no sign of Henry.

A movement in the room made them look up. Katie was standing before them, her face twisted in a frown.

"What's going on, Dad?" Katie asked.

Myra looked at Brody, then wiped her tears.

"Come sit down, Katie," Brody said, patting the couch beside him. "Your grandmother and I were just talking."

Katie crossed her arms over her chest defiantly. "Why are you doing this, Dad?"

Myra was confused. "Katie, what do you mean?"

"You're still going on about how sick you are?" Katie asked, glaring at her father. "Why do you want to upset Grandma so much?"

"Katie, I'm just telling her about the radiation exposure. You know how sick I've been –"

"With the flu!" Katie said, raising her voice. "It's just the flu, Dad! You know it is."

"Katie, I don't think this is the flu," Myra began. "I think this is serious."

"Grandma, he's just doing this for attention!" Katie

insisted. "Just like he says I do stuff for attention. He just caught some bug! He's going to be better in a couple of days!"

Brody reached his arm out toward his daughter, trying to take her hand. But the teenager turned away. In a blur, she began to run up the stairs.

"Katie!" Myra exclaimed, shocked by her granddaughter's behavior.

Katie stormed away. The sound of her bedroom door being slammed made Myra jump.

Myra started to stand up. "I'll go talk to her."

Brody shook his head. "No, just let her go. She needs to cool off."

Myra looked at him, bewildered. "What was that all about?"

"Have you forgotten what it's like to raise teenagers?" Brody asked with a tired smile.

"But why did she say you're not really sick?" Myra asked.

"She doesn't want to believe she could lose her father," Brody said, slumping back into the couch. "This is how she's dealing with that possibility. Denying it. Turning her anger about the situation into anger at me."

Myra thought about that. "I guess so. But still, that's no way to talk to you!"

"No, it's not. I'll try to talk to her later. But for now, she needs to be on her own."

Myra nodded, then swallowed. "Do you think she'll still help me search for Henry?" She almost whispered her husband's name.

"Of course," Brody said. "She'll be back down here in a few minutes anyway. She doesn't have any food up there, after all. And I'm sure she'll want to help you search for her grandpa."

Myra turned her head away so Brody wouldn't see the tears forming in her eyes once again. "Okay, I'd appreciate that. And we can cover a lot more ground on the bicycles." Her voice started to shake, and she stopped talking. She pushed herself to her feet and started to move toward the kitchen again.

"Mom?"

She turned back to look at him.

"Everything's going to be okay," Brody said. "You're going to find Dad. He's out there somewhere. I know it. And Heather, and Annie. You'll see them all again."

Myra nodded, the tears rolling down her cheeks. She patted her son's hand. "You're right, Brody. Everything's going to be okay."

She gave his hand a squeeze, then returned to the kitchen. She wanted to lose herself in banal tasks. She wanted to focus on something she could actually accomplish. Everything else in her life seem to be spinning out of control.

5

SUNDAY 1:03 P.M. - SOUTHWESTERN VIRGINIA

Heather Walsh had been riding for hours, since the early morning when she had left the cornfield in a frenzy. She was already exhausted, but she had many more miles to cover before reaching her parents' house in Northeastern Tennessee.

The more she rode, the more she was filled with dread. She saw destruction everywhere – homes and businesses vandalized and looted, vehicles stripped and smashed. She had already seen two dead bodies on the edge of a larger town today. They had been stabbed, and they lay in a pool of blood. Her stomach turned as she recalled the gory sight.

She didn't have enough food or water, and her hunger and thirst were catching up to her. She thought constantly about a cool bottle of water. And the exertion of riding the bike made her more ravenous than ever. Even with careful rationing of her supplies, she only had a little water and some dried fruit remaining.

She was coming upon another small town. It looked fairly quiet as she rode the highway downhill past deserted gas stations and houses.

Heather had mostly avoided stopping in populated areas. Ever since the EMP and the nuclear attacks, her faith in humanity had been at an all-time low. This was not a time she wanted to be dealing with strangers.

But her stomach was painfully empty, and her mouth was parched. There could easily be a delay in getting to her parents' house. And if she arrived any later than expected, dehydration would become more and more likely.

She came to a gas station. A few abandoned cars were scattered around the parking lot, and the station had been broken into. The glass door was shattered. But there was no one around. It looked like it had been empty for a while. The nearest building was a house in the lot directly behind the gas station. The house looked empty as well.

She steered her bike into the parking lot of the gas station. Maybe she could find some food left behind from the looters. If she was quick, she could get in and out without seeing anyone.

Heather coasted toward the front door of the store, then applied her brakes, skidding to a stop. She looked inside the store. It was destroyed, but empty of people. Turning back toward the street, she took one last look around the sleepy little town.

No one in sight.

Hopping off her bike, she leaned it against the front wall of the store and stepped inside.

The shelves had been cleared of merchandise. The doors to the refrigerated section had been torn off their hinges, and those shelves were empty as well. Heather's heart sank. With a lump in her throat, she walked up and down the aisles of the store, searching for any forgotten items.

Then, something caught her eye. A small cabinet underneath the coffee station, tucked in the corner near an end cap. The cabinet door was closed. Maybe the looters had overlooked it.

She opened the little cabinet door to find a small supply of juice boxes. It had apparently been an overflow area, and to Heather's luck, no one had seen it before her. She quickly grabbed the juice boxes, stuffing most of them in her backpack.

She had planned to take whatever she could find and leave, but her physical needs overcame her. She began to frantically tear open one of the juice boxes and guzzle its contents. The sweet liquid revived her almost instantly, and she moved on to a second and third box.

With the cabinet cleared out, she turned to leave. But near the front door, the corner of a bright blue wrapper caught her eye. Peering underneath the newspaper display, she spotted a small bag of cookies that had fallen into a little nook. Reaching into the tight space, she grabbed the package and pulled it out.

All her willpower flew out the window, and she wasn't able to save the cookies for later. She tore into the package and began shoveling the food into her mouth, eating it greedily.

Heather had been in the store several minutes now, and she was getting nervous about being in one place for too long. What if someone down the road noticed her bike and decided to come check it out?

Still dumping cookie crumbs into her mouth, she headed toward the door.

With her mouth still full and her spirits lifted a bit, she grabbed the bike's handlebars and swung her leg over the frame.

Just as she was about to push off and ride away, the sound of a child screaming pierced the air.

Heather felt her chest contract as she listened to the blood-curdling scream echo through the valley.

The scream had come from nearby, probably from the house behind the gas station. Heather felt the urge to get on the bike and ride away, but she heard the voice again.

"No! No! Help! Somebody help me!"

Heather felt the tightening move from her chest up to her throat. There was a little girl back there. And she needed help.

With shaking hands, Heather withdrew the knife she kept in her backpack. She set the pack down beside the bike, then began to walk toward the edge of the building.

What are you doing? Get out of here! Go!

A big part of her wanted to leave, and chided her for thinking she could help. But she couldn't just let a child get hurt.

Heather silently inched toward the edge of the wall, then looked around the corner of the building, toward the house behind the station.

In the front yard of the rundown wooden home, a large man was wrestling with a little girl of about eight or nine. She tried to run away from him, but he grabbed her as she squirmed, trying to wrest free of his reach. It was clear the two weren't related – they looked nothing alike. And even if he was some relation to the girl, the child was obviously terrified.

The girl slapped at him, her eyes wide with horror. Again, she screamed out for help.

"Leave me alone, leave me alone! Help, please!"

For just a moment, Heather hesitated. What could she

do to help? The man was much larger than Heather. There was no way she could overpower him.

But then, there was no way she could leave this child alone to be hurt by him.

The man finally scooped the girl up and began to carry her off in his arms. They were headed toward the front door of the house. The girl continued screaming and struggling.

Heather moved quickly, careful to keep quiet as possible. She ran lightly across the rear parking lot of the gas station, crossed an alley, then entered the front yard of the house.

Her heart thudded out of control in her chest. What would she do once she reached him? How would she make her move?

Though her mind was at a loss, somehow her body knew what to do. Clenching the knife as she neared the man, she covered the last few feet in a charge. Watching him carry that little girl so roughly, Heather was filled with rage. He wanted to hurt that child.

Heather wasn't going to let him. Her anger fueled her movements, but she was careful to keep quiet. She gained on him as he scaled the top step of the porch. He opened the front door and was crossing the entrance with the girl when Heather lunged at him.

The little girl saw her first.

Heather plunged the knife into the man's lower back, just to his side. It was a sharp, long blade, and it went deep. Heather was surprised at how easily it pierced his flesh.

The man let out an enraged roar. He let go of the little girl, who fell to the floor inside the house.

Heather reached for the knife still jutting from the man's side, but he whipped around before she could.

His fiery gaze landed on Heather. Confusion flashed

across his face for a moment. Then he understood, and his eyes widened in anger.

Heather took a step back. Keeping her eyes on the man, she nearly fell down the porch steps. The man's face went dark as he looked at her for a moment.

Finally, he made a sudden movement, lunging at Heather.

The sound of her scream filled the quiet town.

6

Myra pedaled the bicycle furiously, trying to keep up with her granddaughter.

They were on a Forest Service road, traveling on bicycles through the hilly, wooded land. Myra rode on Brody's bike. It was too big for her, but she was happy to have it. They were able to cover much more ground than Myra had on foot. Brody was resting back at the house, having assured his mother that he would be okay alone.

Another day searching for Henry, Myra's missing husband. Every so often, Myra would begin to lose hope of ever finding him. After all, he had been gone for over three days. But every time she found herself despairing, she pushed those thoughts away. She was going to find him.

Katie disappeared over the next hill. Myra panted to catch her breath. If she was constantly trying to keep up with the teenager, she wouldn't have time to search through the woods surrounding the road.

"Katie, slow down!" Myra called.

Myra struggled over the hill, scanning both sides of the road for any break in the dense green forest. At the crest of the hill, she saw Katie below. Katie watched as Myra coasted down the hill and came to a stop beside her.

"You're going too fast for me, kiddo," Myra said as she struggled to catch her breath.

"Sorry, Grandma," Katie said. "I'll try to slow down." Katie looked around, pushing her long, red hair behind her shoulders.

"Do you think we'll find him out here?" Katie asked in a small voice.

Myra smiled. "Of course I do. He's out here somewhere. He probably twisted an ankle trying to walk back after his truck died."

Katie nodded, then looked away. Myra saw the worry on the girl's face. The older woman wrapped her arms around Katie, pulling her close. Katie let herself be embraced without pushing away, which Myra took as a good sign.

"It's okay, sweetie," Myra said. "We're going to find your granddad."

Katie looked up at her and drew a deep breath. "But . . . what about water? He's been out here for a few days, hasn't he?"

Myra swallowed. "He always takes a big Thermos of coffee in his truck wherever he goes. I reckon he's made it back to his truck and has been rationing that coffee. It would be enough to keep him alive for a few days. But we have to find him today, all right?"

Katie sniffed and nodded. "Are you ready?"

"Ready."

They took off on their bikes down the dirt road. Katie seemed a bit more open to talking than she'd been back at the house, so Myra decided to broach another difficult subject.

"You know your father loves you very much, right?" Myra began.

"I know."

"I – I want you to be prepared, Katie. He's very sick."

Katie frowned. "I'd rather not talk about this."

"I know this is difficult for you. I know you care about him."

"Dad's going to be fine. It's just the flu."

"But Katie, he was out there after the bomb –"

"Yeah, he was worried about some other little kid. If he had cared about me, he would've stayed at home." Katie began to pedal faster.

"You mean the world to him! He was just trying to do the right thing and help that little boy who didn't have anyone. It doesn't mean he didn't care about you!"

"But he should've stayed with me. This is all his fault. If he had cared about me, he wouldn't have gone out there. And he wouldn't have gotten sick!"

She began to race ahead, pushing her bike toward the curve on the road.

"Katie, wait!"

Myra watched as her granddaughter disappeared around the curve on the mountain bike. Seeing the child so upset pained Myra. Brody had been right – this was Katie's way of dealing with an impossible situation. Rather than face the possibility of losing her dad, Katie was lashing out at everyone around her.

Myra steered her bike down the road. She didn't try to catch up with Katie this time. Best to let her cool off alone.

If only I had a magic wand.

Everything in Myra's life seemed to be falling apart, and there was nothing she could do about it. Her husband was missing, her son possibly dying. And she didn't know where her daughters were. Or even if they were alive.

No. Don't think the worst.

She couldn't let herself fall into despair. There was too much work to do. She might not be able to fix all of the problems right now, but she had to keep trying. She had to do everything she could to find her family and keep them safe.

"Grandma!" Katie called suddenly. The alarm in Katie's voice sent a chill down Myra's spine. "Come quick!"

Myra's heart began to pound. She pedaled quickly, approaching the curve in the road. She steeled herself against what she might see.

Finally, she rounded the curve and saw Katie standing on the road, still straddling her bike.

Henry's truck was parked on the side of the road.

7
―――

The two shooters pummeled the roof with bullets.

Jack slid on his belly to the side. One of the shooters never stopped, but the second one paused at last.

Jack lifted his rifle and aimed toward the first shooter. Gritting his teeth, he unleashed a torrent of rounds. First at one target, then the other.

Finally, all was quiet. A pool of blood expanded on the ground behind the garbage dumpster. The second shooter lay face-up in the parking lot, his eyes glazing over.

With his heart pounding, Jack began to descend the ladder.

His ears rang, and the voices in the distance were muted and fuzzy. But he could tell they were increasing in strength. More guards were on their way.

His eyes watered, mixing with the sweat running down from his forehead. Several feet above the ground, he jumped from the ladder, hitting the ground with a jolt.

He moved toward the first downed man – the first guard he had shot, who he'd mistaken for dead at first. Jack snatched up his AR-15 and found some ammo in the guy's pocket. The man wore a Glock in a holster. With trembling hands, Jack unfastened the holster and snatched it up as well.

Jack ran to the second man behind the dumpster, grabbing his Bushmaster rifle and a small supply of ammo. As he grabbed the things off the dead body, he heard footsteps approaching from the front of the building, coming from the west.

With two of the rifles slung over his shoulder and the third in his arms, Jack took off running.

The footsteps pounded the pavement several yards away, then came to a stop at one of the guards.

Jack tore through the parking lot, heading to the south. He looked frantically to the left and right, his tunnel vision shaky and confused.

Which way, which way?

Voices made their way through his fuzzy hearing to him. People were nearby, coming from the left. He veered to the right, running between a cluster of abandoned cars at the edge of the lot.

He turned down an alley between two large apartment buildings.

There was someone on his trail. He heard them knock over a garbage can in the parking lot behind him. They weren't yet in the alley, but they would get there soon.

And once they got there, Jack would be spotted.

The alley opened up into a large road. Jack heard the sound of work being done in the next block – rhythmic clanging of hammers and other tools. If he ran out to that road, he would be seen by a work crew – and their guards.

He was trapped.

Up ahead, a fire escape ladder gave access to the apartment building on the right. Without hesitation, Jack began to scale the ladder.

His only hope was that could get inside to one of the windows.

He had to hurry. At any moment, the guard could enter the alley and shoot him.

He made it to the first floor. The window was closed. Jack pulled on it. It opened. He pushed the rifles inside, then squeezed himself through the small opening.

Silently, he waited inside the room. A moment later, the footsteps grew louder as a guard entered the alley down below.

It was a young man with a shotgun, dressed in an ill-fitting police uniform that was typical of members of the gang. Jack waited as the guy got close to the ladder.

If the guard climbed the ladder, Jack could take him. Jack was in the position of advantage – perched up high out of sight. He wasn't worried about this guard as much as he worried about giving his location away.

Firing a gun in that alley would send dozens of guards running. They would enter the apartment building, trapping him where he couldn't get out.

Jack held his breath.

The guard kept running. Somehow, he didn't even look at the ladder. He was so focused on the road ahead that he didn't even stop in the alley.

The guard's dumb error had bought Jack some time, but he wasn't yet out of harm's way. Far from it.

In fact, he didn't even know if this apartment building was empty.

The room was dark, and at first he couldn't see anything. As his eyes adjusted to the darkness, he looked around.

The room had been ransacked, torn apart for anything

of value. But it didn't look like anyone was living in the apartment. Oscar's gang hadn't used it as one of their prison rooms.

Jack moved through the rooms quietly. It was a shabby one-bedroom apartment. Someone had lived in it just a few days ago. Now, that person was either dead or enslaved.

Jack returned to the window, looking out at the alley below. For several minutes, he didn't see any movement out there.

Moving quickly, he looked over the weapons he had taken. He reloaded the rifles. He would have liked more ammo, but it would have to do. He adjusted the Glock in its holster, glad to not have to carry a gun in his waistband for a change.

He spent several nervous minutes pacing around the room and keeping an eye on the alley below.

The work crew on the next block were still at it, banging around with hand tools. He could hear the guards supervising them, giving them orders.

He would have to make a move soon. He had to find Brent and Naomi without getting shot.

And that meant going deeper into the gang's territory.

8

SUNDAY, 12:41 P.M. - WHITE ROCK

Naomi stood her shovel upright and perched it in a crack in the ground. She leaned against it, shielding her face from the sun for just a moment.

Nearby, a woman glanced at her. Looking quickly away and back at her own work, the fellow inmate spoke to Naomi under her breath. "Don't let them see you resting, dear."

Naomi looked over at the nearest guard. Sure enough, the guard had noticed Naomi leaning against her shovel. The guard was headed her way. Naomi quickly drove the tool into the dry earth once more.

"That's right, 156," the guard hissed. "Don't let me catch you slacking off again."

Naomi's eyes darted up toward the guard as the woman walked away. The guard was a tall woman in her thirties with black hair and skin so pale it looked like it had never seen the light of day. The woman wore a large sun hat, paired with some kind of uniform that looked like it had once belonged to a park ranger. The other prisoners jokingly called the woman Morticia.

The prisoners had grown adept at communicating in brief moments while they worked. The women had to speak to each other in little snippets, without looking at each other, and without moving their lips. The guards had forbidden any talking while the prisoners were out of their rooms.

Naomi was being kept prisoner along with hundreds of other women. She hadn't seen Jack or Brent since those *people* had separated them at the headquarters.

Naomi remembered how terrible that first day had been. She had been taken through the town, past several blocks, to the women's dormitory. The women were kept in a budget motel. The female guards had led Naomi to a room on the second floor and locked her in there alone. Naomi sat there in the dark for a couple hours, on a bed that had already been slept in.

Naomi sat there despairing. What had they done to Jack as punishment after he'd called the leader, Oscar, a coward? Had they killed him? Was Brent still alive?

How had her life so completely deteriorated in under a week?

Finally, a female guard unlocked the door.

"Time to work, 156!" the woman barked.

Naomi looked up at the woman, who clutched a shotgun in her muscled arms. The woman had dyed her hair green, and she sneered at Naomi in disgust.

"You're too scrawny to do much work, but I bet you can learn to dig a hole," she spat.

Naomi felt tears brimming in her eyes. So these people had captured her and the only two people Naomi had left in the world – and they were going to force them to work?

Naomi felt herself sinking into a dark hole. She was trapped in a nightmare, and she didn't know how to wake up.

There was no escape from these people, and no one was coming to rescue her. Jack was probably dead, or would be soon, judging from the gang leaders' reaction when Jack had defied them. And Brent was sweet, but not exactly the rescuer type. It was hopeless. And she had lost her mother, the most important person in her life. What did she even have to live for anymore?

Naomi decided to just give up.

She didn't want to work for these people. She didn't want to further their cause. They would kill her eventually, anyway.

Naomi closed her eyes and waited.

"Are you deaf? I said it's time to work!" the guard said, raising her voice.

Naomi didn't respond.

The guard was losing her patience. She crossed the room in long strides and stood before Naomi. She grabbed Naomi's chin and lifted it upward.

"What's the matter with you, 156? You just gonna sit here crying all day? I'll give you something to cry about!"

Naomi braced herself. A moment later, she felt the woman's hand strike her face.

"Get up!" the guard screamed.

Naomi slumped over, letting her body go limp.

The guard shifted the shotgun to her left arm. With her free hand, she grabbed Naomi under her arm and pulled her off the bed. Naomi felt her body crash to the floor. She cringed from the impact on her bottom and hip.

"Around here, we all have to work! This is what happens

Survive the End

when you don't work!" the guard roared. She kicked Naomi in the gut. Naomi curled up, groaning in agony.

The guard grabbed Naomi by her hair and lifted her head off the floor. "You lie there and think about what you're going to do," the woman said. "I'll be back to see what you've decided."

The woman gave her one final slap across her face, harder this time, and let her head hit the carpet before she turned and left the room.

Naomi lay there for a long time.

Her stomach was aching from the guard's kick, and Naomi's face and backside hurt as well. But what else could she do? She didn't want to spend the rest of her days helping these evil people build an empire. She couldn't fight them, and she had lost hope that there was anyone left who could save her.

She would just let them beat her to death.

Finally, she heard the door open. She swallowed the lump in her throat and felt tears spill from her eyes again.

This would be the end.

It wasn't the green-haired guard standing in the doorway this time. It was a guard with black hair.

I guess they sent someone else to finish the job, Naomi thought to herself as she lifted her head off the floor and watched the new guard step inside the room.

But there was another woman behind her. A middle-aged woman with short brown hair walked inside. She was sweaty, and her skin was sunburned. Naomi could tell from her body language that she was another prisoner.

This new woman walked inside and sat on the second bed, looking down at Naomi on the floor.

The guard slammed the door shut and walked with

heavy boots across the room. Naomi stared at the boots inches from her eyes.

"You ready to work now, 156?"

Naomi looked up at the guard who frowned down at her and clutched a big rifle. Then Naomi closed her eyes. Maybe they would shoot her instead of beating her this time. Then it would be over faster.

Naomi felt a heavy boot slam into her belly again.

"What the hell's wrong with you?" the woman asked in an amused voice. "You want to just go out like this?"

She kicked her in the knees this time. Naomi whimpered in pain. With her eyes closed, Naomi heard the woman lift her rifle up in the air, preparing to bring it down against her head. Naomi cringed, waiting for the final blow to take her life.

"No, stop!" a new voice rang out.

Naomi gritted her teeth, waiting for the new pain to come anyway.

"Don't hit her anymore! Let me talk to her. I can make her work!"

Naomi opened her eyes to see the other prisoner, who was standing now, pleading with the guard.

"You need more workers for the latrine project! I can get her to work for you!"

The guard looked at the older prisoner, then down at Naomi in disgust.

"Fine. You've got a half-hour," the guard said. Then she spun on her heels and left the room, locking the door behind her.

The older woman knelt at Naomi's side and lightly touched her shoulder. "Are you okay?"

Naomi stared at her. "Why did you do that?"

The woman didn't answer.

"I wanted her to kill me," Naomi said, her voice shaking. "I'm not going to be a prisoner here!"

The woman brushed Naomi's long brown hair out of her face, then rested her hand on her shoulder. Somehow, the woman's touch made Naomi feel a sense of relief. She began to weep where she lay on the floor.

"It's all right," the woman said, patting her hand. She reached over toward her bed and produced a small towel. The woman pressed it against Naomi's forehead. Naomi hadn't realized it, but she was bleeding from where the first guard had hit her.

"My name's Joanne. What's yours?"

"Naomi."

Joanne helped her to sit up, then looked at the wound on her forehead.

"I think it's stopped bleeding. Are you hurt anywhere else? Is your stomach okay?"

Naomi groaned as she moved. "I'm hurt all over. But I'm going to live, unfortunately. At least for now."

Joanne tsked. "No, you can't let them keep hitting you. You have to stay alive, Naomi."

Naomi sighed. "Why? So I can be their slave until they decide to kill all of us?"

"No," Joanne said as she sat on the floor beside Naomi. "You work for them so you can stay alive. But it won't be forever. We'll find a way to get to someplace safe."

Naomi shook her head. "There's no way out of here! They've got guards all over the place. How do you expect to make it out of here in one piece?"

"I don't know that yet. I just know that if we do what they say –"

"You mean work for these monsters?" Naomi shook her

head bitterly. "What's the point of that? What kind of life is that?"

"If we do what they say and don't give them any trouble," Joanne continued patiently, "we can come up with a plan. We can watch them, find their weaknesses."

Naomi scoffed.

"Everyone's got a weakness. We just don't know what theirs is yet," Joanne said. "It might take some time, but I know we can find a way out of here."

Naomi shook her head. "I'm not so optimistic. I've already lost everything that matters. So I don't want to keep on fighting." She wiped away the tears rolling down her cheeks. "I don't have anything to live for anymore."

Joanne took her hand and held it in her own. "As long as you're alive, there's hope. You have to keep on living, no matter what you lost."

Naomi frowned. "It's not what I lost, but who. When you lose the most important person in your life, it's hard to go on fighting."

Joanne was quiet for a moment. Finally, she sighed. "I know it is. But it's what they would have wanted us to do."

Naomi looked at her. "Did you lose someone too?"

"My daughter," Joanne said, looking away. "She had just turned seventeen last week. And now..."

Her voice broke, and she stopped.

"I'm so sorry," Naomi said. "Was it... them?"

Joanne nodded. "In our own house. We were trying to get away from them. Maddie was climbing out her bedroom window, and they – they shot her. My poor baby! I still can't believe she's gone."

Joanne shook her head sadly, staring off into the distance. Naomi felt her own pain surge as the two sat in silence. Finally, Joanne sniffed and looked at her.

"Who did you lose?"

"My mother," Naomi whispered.

Joanne pulled Naomi close, and they were quiet for a while.

"Your mother would have wanted you to live, Naomi," Joanne said. "And Maddie wouldn't want me to just give up, either. We have to do it for them."

Before Naomi could answer, the sound of a key in the doorknob startled them. Joanne got up and sat on her own bed just before the dark-haired guard appeared.

The guard entered the room and looked at Naomi expectantly.

"What's it going to be, 156?"

Naomi glanced at Joanne, then up at the guard. She drew a breath.

"I'll work."

"Good choice," the guard said, then ushered the women out the door with a sharp motion of her rifle.

That afternoon, Naomi had begun work digging a latrine with the other women. She quickly got into the routine of the operation, and learned never to talk during worktime.

She glanced over at Joanne, digging at the dry earth nearby. If it hadn't been for her new friend, Naomi would have already been dead.

She still wasn't convinced they would find a way out. But Joanne had convinced her to not give up hope just yet. Still, though, Naomi knew she couldn't do this indefinitely. She didn't have it in her. She'd either have to find a way to freedom, or die trying.

9

The man wrapped his arms around Annie, and pulled her down. She hit the ground hard.

"Get the hell away from me!" she yelled at him.

Annie elbowed him in his chest with all her might. She pulled herself away a few inches, getting some traction on the cedar log nearby.

He grabbed at her legs. She kicked him in the face, but not hard enough. He pulled at her legs, causing her to slip in the mud and fall to the ground again.

"I'm not going to hurt you!" he said in a pleading voice. "I just want a friend!"

The way he said the word *friend* made Annie shudder. He was either insane or as high as a kite.

They struggled a bit more. Finally, she got her arm free and elbowed him in the eye.

He recoiled, his hands flying to his face.

He looked at her with an expression of shock and surprise, then he turned and ran inside the house.

"You'll pay for this!" he yelled just before slamming the door shut.

Annie scrambled to her feet. Judging from his dilated pupils and the erratic way he moved, the guy was clearly strung out on drugs. She didn't want to wait around and see how he would make her pay.

She ran toward the driveway. But something caught her eye – a stable. It was behind and to the left of the house.

She looked back at the house. The man could emerge any moment with a gun. She knew it was a risk. Maybe it was even stupid. But she had to do it.

She took off running toward the stable. As she got closer, she heard movement inside the structure.

Inside the stall was a beautiful, chestnut American Quarter Horse.

Annie felt her heart leap for joy. She stepped inside the stable and approached the animal.

"It's okay, it's okay," she murmured soothingly to the horse. "Do you want to go for a ride?"

The horse snorted and stepped toward the gate. Annie looked at the horse – a mare. She seemed tame and gentle. Annie stroked her nose, and the horse seemed glad for the company.

Annie looked back at the house. Still no sign of the man.

She grabbed the saddle from the hook on the wall and, leaning over the gate, positioned it on the horse.

"How's that?" Annie whispered. She hoped she was doing this right, but she didn't have much time to make sure.

She spun around, looking through the stable, and her eyes landed on some ropes and a harness.

Bingo.

Then she opened the gate. The horse, already fully accepting of Annie's presence, waited patiently for her commands.

She mounted the horse, then clicked her tongue. The horse took off at a slow trot and left the stable.

Annie urged the horse faster with her legs, and the horse picked up speed.

They covered the distance in front of the house at a gallop. Annie looked back at the house. The man didn't appear in the door, but she heard a crashing noise from within the home.

Annie felt the panic rise up inside. Was he coming after her now that she was escaping with the horse?

She urged the mare faster, squeezing her legs around the horse's trunk, and holding on tight. She looked over her shoulder, watching for the man to emerge.

But the horse carried her all the way to the highway, kicking up dust behind them.

And he still hadn't reappeared.

Once they were on the highway again, Annie felt she could breathe a little. Looking down at her hands, she saw she was shaking. She took a deep breath. She was still alive.

"Good girl," she said, patting the horse's shiny brown coat. "You're going to save us."

The horse seemed to enjoy the ride. She, like Annie, had been yearning to move. She carried Annie up and over the hill. Annie got one last look at the house below before it was out of sight.

"Hang on, Charlotte," Annie muttered under her breath. "Almost there."

Halfway up the next hill, gunshots rang out across the countryside. Annie felt herself freeze up inside, even though the sun was warming up the area. Her mouth was suddenly dry as her heart sped up in her chest.

The gunfire had come from the east, and it could have easily come from Dan's .22.

10

Charlotte shifted in her seat, mindful of the bullet wounds.

She still couldn't believe she was alive.

At least something had gone right in the disaster that had been the past few days. Annie had kept her from bleeding to death.

But now, Charlotte had something new to worry about.

Annie had been gone too long.

Charlotte watched the sun rise higher in the sky. Each minute that Annie was gone, Charlotte's uneasiness grew. There were a million things that could go wrong. And since the attacks on Austin, everything that *could* go wrong, *did*.

What would Charlotte do if Annie never returned? She couldn't go looking for her friend – not in her current state. Her throat started to tighten as she thought of all the possibilities. She was afraid for Annie – and herself. And Charlotte was the only one with a weapon.

Charlotte looked down at Dan's .22 in her lap. She had screwed up the day before. She'd been too afraid to shoot

Harvey when she'd had her chance. And she had paid the price for her hesitation.

She ran her finger down the shiny surface of the gun. She had never touched one before yesterday. Charlotte had never expected to be in a situation anything like this.

She sighed and looked out at the road to the west, hoping to see Annie's figure appear on the horizon.

Please hurry. Please be okay.

She leaned her head back in the seat. Overhead, a buzzard circled in the sky.

Maybe he's waiting for his supper. Harvey and I probably look like a sure thing.

As she watched the bird fly overhead, she heard a rustling sound behind her.

Instantly, a wave of fear spread through her body.

Harvey was waking up.

Momentarily forgetting about her injuries, she turned around in her seat too quickly. Pain seared through her torso. But that sensation was soon forgotten.

She looked in horror as Harvey struggled against the rope.

He looked up at her. Their eyes locked for a second. Charlotte saw the rage and darkness in him.

"You tied me up! I can't believe this shit!"

And he worked furiously at the knot at his wrists. He muttered, "You'll pay for this. Oh, you'll pay all right."

Charlotte swung her legs out of the car. Trembling, she pushed herself to her feet and turned to face him.

She watched, horrified, as Harvey got his hands free. He glanced up at her, scowling, as he pushed himself up to sit in the grass. Then he started working on the knot at his ankles.

"We both know you ain't gonna use that gun," he said, keeping his eyes on his work at the rope. "Don't even front."

Charlotte took a breath.

She looked at the gun, flicked the safety off, and brought it up with both hands.

Harvey glanced up at her again. This time, he couldn't hide the fear in his eyes. He kept fumbling with the knot, his hands shaking.

Charlotte aimed right for the center of his chest. She exhaled and pulled the trigger.

11

The man leapt toward Heather, reaching out for her in a furor.

Heather stepped to the side, just dodging his grasp. His arm brushed against her side as he stumbled. He nearly fell down the steps, but caught himself.

Before Heather could react, he turned and grabbed her. He grunted as he pulled on her arm.

With her free hand, she withdrew the knife in a sudden movement.

She tried to stab him again in his belly, but he grabbed her arm as she made the movement. Heather's hand was clenched tightly around the knife. She didn't let go.

"Give me that!" he roared.

The man grabbed her arms, twisting them around behind her. Enraged, she tried to jerk free.

She kicked him, then wrenched her right arm away from him.

Without hesitation, she plunged the knife in his thigh.

He screamed in agony, cursing at the top of his lungs. He released her arm and looked down at the wound, his hands shaking. His mouth opened, and a strange wailing noise began to flow out of his mouth.

Behind her, the little girl scrambled to her feet. She scurried off the porch, unnoticed by both Heather and the man.

Heather jerked the knife out of his body again. She stood in a defensive stance, waiting for him to make his next move.

The man took a step toward Heather, then stumbled.

Heather backed away, keeping her eyes on him. Finally, he fell to his knees on the porch. His hands covered the hole in his leg. Blood gushed out from the wound, making his hands slick and deep red.

Heather turned around to see the girl was gone. Heather jumped off the porch, then ran into the yard. She saw the little girl running down the street, away from the house as fast as her legs could carry her.

"Wait!" Heather called.

She ran a few steps down the road behind the girl and called after her once more.

"Wait! I'm not going to hurt you!"

But the little girl was long gone. Terrified from the encounter, she ran down the street without looking back.

Heather came to a stop. She had done what she could. She couldn't chase after the girl. Heather hoped the child had a safe home to return to.

She ran across the front yard of the house again, expecting to see the man lying on the porch, reeling from his injuries.

A tidal wave of fear coursed through her as she glanced over at the porch.

The man was gone.

Heather looked around in all directions, spinning in a circle in the yard. The man was nowhere to be found.

She broke into a sprint across the tall grass in front of the house. As she reached the parking lot, she looked behind her. She saw what she had missed before – a trail of blood across the porch of the house. The man had made his way inside the home.

He was either bleeding to death inside the house, or he was getting his gun.

Heather rounded the corner of the gas station and grabbed her bike. In her panic, she lost her balance as she pushed off. Tumbling to the ground, her hands and left arm broke the fall. Shaking from fright, she scrambled to her feet and mounted the bike again.

Suddenly, the sleepy town seemed full of eyes that were watching her. She feared that someone might be waiting for her out of sight, ready to pounce. And most of all, she feared the man would emerge from his front door at any moment and open fire.

She raced through the front lot of the gas station on her bicycle and began to pedal down the highway.

Her heart was pounding so quickly that nausea began to overtake her. Adrenaline flooded her system, making her confused and panicked. She glanced behind her shoulder, almost expecting to see the man coming after her.

She continued through the small town, passing block after block of homes and businesses. Most of them were empty, but she saw a few people scattered here and there. Suddenly paranoid, she was terrified of them all. She pressed onward, not wanting to be detained any longer in the town.

Finally, she made it to the southern outskirts of the town, and then to an unpopulated area. Once again on a deserted stretch of highway, her panic did not subside. Instead, the desertion of the area seemed to heighten her anxiety. She continued to pedal furiously, trying to shake the feeling that someone was following her. She knew it was unlikely the man was on her trail, but she couldn't help looking over her shoulder again and again.

Her heart pounded as she glanced at the thick woods surrounding the road. The forest seemed to be a wall, hemming her in on both sides. She felt her heart beat faster. It was becoming difficult to breathe.

What if she never made it to Tennessee? What if she made it, but her family were missing – or dead?

Maybe she'd never see any of them again.

Fear took her over more completely now. She felt a chill, despite her exertion.

In a matter of days, the world had turned dark and unwelcoming. The attacks on the nation had torn apart the fabric of society. Everyone's morals seemed to have collapsed. Not even the government had been able to protect its citizens from a devastating national disaster.

Heather was all alone.

Her panic increasing, she felt herself toeing the line of hyperventilation. The muscles of her hands, deprived of oxygen, began to contract into claws around her handlebars. Her vision was quickly blurring, the road and the trees becoming distorted shapes.

She pushed the bicycle faster, glancing behind her once more. Any moment now, she expected the man to appear on the road, chasing her to exact his revenge. Her only chance at survival was to get as far away as fast as she could.

12

Jack watched the alley from the apartment. No other guards had run through after the first one.

Where are they?

The lack of activity on the street below was unsettling. He almost would have preferred to see the guards searching for him. As it was, the relative calmness outside the apartment had him wondering what they were up to.

The anxious minutes in that room had a distinct feeling of a calm before a storm.

Were they waiting for him outside, lulling him into a false sense of security to make him think he could leave unnoticed, then ambush him?

There was only one way to find out.

He didn't risk everything by taking out the five guards and re-entering their territory only to turn tail and run.

He'd have to leave the shelter and go out looking for Brent and Naomi.

Gathering his weapons, he shot one more glance down

below. Still nothing happening in the alley. As tempting as it was to descend the fire escape ladder, he left it behind and headed toward the front door of the apartment.

He would have to go out another way. The alley opened up onto a main street, where a work crew was supervised by several guards. And the other end of the alley pointed toward the road he had just crossed, where the men had been on his trail.

Opening the front door, he checked the hallway of the building. Empty, except for scattered debris of the looters.

Jack emerged from the apartment and found the stairwell. Light filtered in from a skylight, illuminating his path down to the first floor. Quietly and cautiously, he opened the door to the first floor, walked into the hall, and approached a door with an exit sign.

The door was a side exit out of the building. It was a solid metal door without a window, which meant Jack would walk out of the building blind. But the front door wouldn't work, since it opened onto the main street and well within view of the work crew.

He positioned the rifle just right, then pushed the door open slightly with his foot. He waited and listened for any movement or reaction on the other side, then brought his face up to the crack to look out.

The door opened onto a small street. Other than several useless and abandoned cars lining the side of the road, there was very little cover. Across the street, a large semi was left sprawled across a large parking lot. If he could cross the street and take cover behind that truck, he could get a better view of his surroundings.

This side street was empty, but he could hear the voice of the work crew around the corner on the adjacent street.

One of the guards might spot him, but he had to take the risk.

Jack stepped outside the door and let it shut quietly behind him. He quickly bolted across the street, stepping lightly as he ran. The rifles he wore over his shoulders limited his mobility, but he pressed onward.

He made it to the rear edge of the semi. Panting to catch his breath, he looked around. So far, no one appeared to have seen him. The sounds of the work crew nearby continued.

Jack advanced behind the cover of the truck, which was parked right behind a pharmacy building. Jack peered around the front cabin, looking across the street at the blocks ahead of him to the west.

Several hundred feet to the north and three or four blocks away, a work crew of about five male prisoners stood digging a large hole. Jack spotted two armed men guarding them. He was too far away to make out any distinguishing features of the prisoners.

Could Brent be in that group?

Farther to the south, several people pulled trailers on bicycles. Scattered throughout the area were more armed guards walking through the streets, patrolling the area.

Jack had to find a way to the work crew.

He waited until the closest guard had gotten a good two blocks away on the street facing the pharmacy. Then, holding the rifles close to his body to minimize noise from the clanging metal, he crossed the street and the parking lot on the next block.

He took cover behind a garbage dumpster, surveyed the scene, then crossed the next street. Slowly, he made his way to the edge of another alley. Hiding himself behind an abandoned car, he crouched down and watched the work crew nearby, on the other side of a chain-link fence.

The men were scattered around a large, empty lot. Jack was almost within speaking distance of the closest prisoner, a young man who labored with a shovel. Jack squinted, trying to see the other prisoners.

Brent wasn't there.

Jack fought back frustration. He had chosen the wrong work crew. And now he had gotten himself into a bad situation – he was too close to the guards who might see him trying to leave.

And where would he go? He didn't see any other work crews. The gang's territory was sprawling. Brent could be working on any of several dozen blocks to the south, east, or west.

The guard inside the lot was slowly making his way around the fenced-in area, supervising the men digging. When he began to make the loop facing away from Jack's end of the lot, Jack made his move.

"Hey!" he hissed at the prisoner on the other side of the fence.

The prisoner startled, then turned to see Jack crouched in the bushes nearby. The young man was confused and stared at Jack for a moment. Then, remembering the risk in stopping work, he began digging again. But he positioned himself to face Jack as he worked.

"What are you doing out there?" the prisoner asked under his breath. "And who the hell are you?"

"Nobody," Jack said. "But I'm looking for someone. Do you know a guy by the name of Brent, early twenties, tall and thin, wears glasses? Maybe you know where they have him working?"

The prisoner glanced at Jack, looking at Jack's obvious injuries and wounds, and the weapons strapped to his body.

"You're that guy who escaped, aren't you?" the prisoner said.

Jack shifted uncomfortably, his eyes flitting up to the guards making their rounds.

"Yeah, I heard the guards talking about that this morning!" the guy said, getting excited. "You killed some of them, didn't you?"

"Listen, I'm just looking for my friend," Jack said, keeping his eyes on the guards. The closest one was nearing the end of his loop through the yard. Soon, he would be turning toward Jack and the prisoner.

"Hey, take me with you," the prisoner whispered. "Get me out of here, please!"

"I can't right now," Jack said. "Sorry."

Jack readied himself, preparing to make a run for it before the guard got too close. The prisoner wasn't going to help him. He probably had never even seen Brent.

"I'll tell!" the prisoner said, growing agitated. "I'll call them over here right now if you don't help me get out!"

"Keep your voice down," Jack hissed.

"Then take me with you!" the prisoner pleaded, talking a little too loudly. He had also stopped digging, which Jack knew would draw the attention of the men in charge. Any second now, the guards would notice the prisoner's disruption and come running.

Keeping to the ground, Jack crept away from the fence. He set out in a low run, breaking away from the cover of the vehicle. Darting between the bushes and trees that lined the fence, he ran to the west.

As he ran, he heard the prisoner's voice again behind him, angry and laced with hysteria.

Was he calling after Jack? Was he alerting the guards of an escaped prisoner's presence?

Either way, the guards might have already spotted him. Jack sprinted toward the next street, half-expecting them to open fire on him at any moment.

13

Myra rode her bicycle toward the truck, glancing at Katie as she approached.

"Is he –" Myra began to ask, then stopped herself.

Katie stood frozen in place, paralyzed with fear as she stared at the truck.

Myra came to a stop a few feet away. The door was closed. She moved her eyes frantically over the cab.

It was empty.

With a trembling hand, she opened the door and looked inside. In the middle console cup holder was Henry's coffee Thermos. A paper bag from the hardware store rested in the passenger seat. There were no keys, yet the doors were unlocked.

Myra suddenly felt dizzy. Without thinking, she dismounted the bike and let it fall over onto the gravel road. She took a few steps away from the truck, then started to look around.

"Don't move," she told Katie. "I want to see if I can find any footprints."

She bent over, looking closely at the gravel road, trying to find any footprints. But the heavy winds the day before had blown the road clean, and she couldn't find any tracks.

Searching for any other kind of sign of where her husband might have gone, she spun around in a circle.

Frustrated, she kicked at the rocks on the road.

"Grandma?" Katie asked. "Are you okay?"

Myra wiped the tears from her eyes, but she didn't turn to look at her granddaughter. Instead, she kept staring at the side of the road, which was hemmed in by the thick forest.

Katie got off her bike, looked in the truck, then went to stand by her grandmother. "Why would he leave his truck here like this?" Katie asked after a long silence.

Myra shook her head. "I don't know, sweetheart. I don't know."

She walked to the woods at the edge of the road and stared at the greenery in front of her.

Katie followed her. "What are you looking for?"

"Broken twigs, snapped branches, trampled saplings. Any disturbance that might be caused by a man walking through here," Myra said. "Can you help me look for something like that?"

"Okay," Katie said as she crouched on the edge of the gravel and studied the land.

Myra walked a few steps away, slowly surveying the scene. Then they crossed to the other side of the road where they repeated the process. They found a few areas that looked like an animal had passed through – broken twigs and torn leaves near the ground. Myra followed the animal paths several yards into the woods, but they always lead nowhere. They could find nothing that looked like a human had walked through.

"Well, at least there's no blood or anything like that," Katie said hopefully.

Myra nodded. She she had been thinking the same thing, though she didn't want to say anything to Katie about it. But as it turned out, Katie was already considering the worst possibility.

They spent a long time looking through the woods surrounding the truck. Next they tried riding their bikes farther down the road in search of some kind of sign of Henry.

But there was nothing. Just the same forest they saw everywhere – mostly undisturbed and bearing no sign of a struggle, or of any human having passed through the area.

Henry had vanished.

But how could this be? Myra asked herself as she tromped through the woods, looking high and low for any abnormality in the landscape. The truck wasn't so far from the house that he couldn't have made his way home on foot the first day. And he knew the area well. There was no risk in him losing his way. Certainly after three days, he should have been home by now.

There was no explanation.

Finally, exhausted and hungry, they decided to turn back home.

Myra's heart ached as she followed Katie on the bike. They had found Henry's truck, but not Henry. The whole thing began to seem hopeless.

It was late afternoon when they got home. They found Brody sitting at the dining room table.

Katie burst in the house, headed straight for the kitchen.

"Any luck?" Brody asked his mother as she dragged herself in the front door.

Myra collapsed in a chair beside Brody. Fighting back

tears, she told him how they had found his truck, but no sign of Henry.

Brody shook his head sadly, grappling with the strange news.

"But he's got to be out there somewhere!" he said, looking out the window. "Maybe it's like you said – he injured himself walking back home."

Myra glanced up at Katie, who was busying herself searching for food in the kitchen. "But his coffee Thermos was there," Myra said in a lowered voice.

"So?" Brody asked.

"That coffee was the only thing he had to drink," Myra said. "If he were trying to make it home on foot, don't you think he would take that with him? It's a long walk home from down that Forest Service road. He would've known to bring something to drink – the only thing he had."

Brody pushed his chair away from the table and stood up. Clasping his hands behind his back, he paced back and forth across the living room.

"Maybe he had something else with him," Brody said hopefully. "Maybe he bought a soda at the hardware store, and he took that with him."

"You know he never drinks soda," Myra said.

"It doesn't matter," Brody said impatiently. "The point is, the coffee Thermos means nothing. He could still be out there."

Myra started to answer, but she stopped herself. She stared at Brody in surprise, noticing all at once his upright posture.

"How are you feeling?" Myra asked.

Brody looked at her. "I'm feeling better, Mom. Much better."

Despite her worry about Henry, Myra felt her face open into smile. She stood up and walked toward her son.

"You look better too," she said, noticing his improved color. "That gray tinge to your skin is gone. And your eyes look clearer, too."

Brody nodded distractedly, still thinking about his father.

"I told you it was just the flu," Katie said with her mouth full. She left the kitchen carrying a plate of food and sat down at the table. "Did you make this chicken, Dad? It's really good."

Myra looked at Katie's plate loaded with chicken, boiled potatoes, and cabbage.

"I hope you don't mind, Mom," Brody said. "I cooked some of the things I found in your freezer."

Myra glanced at the kitchen. Several five-gallon jugs of water had been placed in the corner.

"Oh, and I brought that water up from the basement," Brody said. "Is that all you have? We're going to have to figure something else out for water soon."

Myra stood staring at him with her mouth open. "Brody, you're all better! I – I can't believe it!"

"Yeah, it's really weird," Brody said. "I feel completely back to normal."

"Do you think it was the flu after all?" Myra asked.

Brody shrugged. "Maybe. Or maybe the effects of the radiation were just temporary? I don't know."

Myra threw her arms around him, suddenly overwhelmed with joy. Brody embraced his mother.

"This is such great news, Brody!" Myra exclaimed.

Brody nodded. "I know, Mom. It's a big surprise." He let go of her and crossed into the kitchen.

"It's been awful seeing you so ill," Myra said, watching him. "I'm so relieved. I can't lose you, too."

Myra stopped herself, realizing that she had said too much. She didn't want the others to know how quickly she was losing hope of finding Henry. Despite her best efforts to remain optimistic, seeing the truck abandoned there on the side of the road gave her a bad feeling.

"You haven't lost Dad," Brody said.

"I know," Myra said. "I just . . . I'm worried about him."

Brody grabbed a piece of chicken and popped it in his mouth, then headed to the door.

"You saw his truck just south of the creek, right?" Brody asked.

"Yes, on the old Forest Service Road," Myra said, suddenly feeling uneasy. "Why?"

"I'm going out looking for him on the bike," Brody said hurriedly.

"Now? But it'll be dark soon," Myra protested, glancing at the fading light outside.

"I won't be long," Brody said, stepping through the doorway. "I'm going to search through the woods in that area. See if I can find anything. Lock up behind me. And, Katie, mind your grandmother."

Myra watched helplessly as he headed toward the bike. Everything was happening so fast, and she was still uncertain about her son. "Be careful. And hurry back!"

Myra locked the door, then glanced at Katie, who was finishing up her dinner.

"I told you Dad wasn't dying," Katie said. She shook her head as she stabbed a potato with her fork. "No one ever listens to me."

Myra smiled at her granddaughter, patted her shoulder, then walked to the window. Myra watched her son pedal his bike down the driveway and disappear as he turned right on the highway.

Myra had been swept up in the excitement over seeing Brody's dramatic improvement. But now, a sinking feeling began to settle in.

She had cared for three children through all kinds of sicknesses. She knew that sometimes, illness didn't follow a linear trajectory.

Sometimes, a person felt better for a while before the illness came back in full force.

She watched the front yard as the sunlight waned, making the shadows deeper and longer.

And maybe they weren't even dealing with an illness any of them had ever seen. Maybe the effects of radiation exposure didn't follow any of the rules Myra knew.

14

Jack heard shouting behind him, but he kept running.

He didn't know if the guards had noticed him, or if they were merely yelling at the prisoner to keep working.

Either way, Jack covered the distance in a frenzy.

Darting between parked cars, he crossed the parking lot and emerged onto an empty street. Jack spotted a multi-level parking garage on the next block. He charged forward across the street, heading straight for the garage.

Worry nagged at him as he ran. Maybe he was headed for a trap. Maybe the gang used the garage as part of their operation. The top floor would provide a good vantage point for keeping an eye on the area, which the gang would want.

His eyes darted toward an apartment building to the south – just left of the parking garage. Maybe the apartments would be safer?

If he chose wrong, it would mean everything was over. An image of Annie flashed through his mind.

He had to get home to her.

Jack continued straight toward the parking garage. As he entered the cool darkness of the ground level entrance, he hoped he had chosen wisely.

He came to a brief stop inside the shelter of the garage and looked around before continuing. His steps echoed within the vast expanse. So far, the garage appeared to be empty.

Moving quickly between the rows of parked cars, he caught his breath. He made it to the far wall of the garage, stopped, and looked around.

He crouched behind a large SUV, well hidden from the entrance. If anyone was following him, this place would be about as good as any for a confrontation.

He waited several minutes, breathing in the stale air faintly scented of engine oil.

Finally convinced that no one had followed him to the garage, he got up and walked to the window on the west wall. Off to the left was the apartment building. It was an older construction, five stories, that looked like it had been occupied until recently.

Until Oscar's gang had killed or enslaved the occupants.

Now, it looked empty. The gang must have killed half the town for there to be so many vacant homes.

Downhill and to the right was another abandoned lot, overgrown with invasive weeds. A work crew was occupied digging various holes around the lot. Jack squinted in the sun, looking at each prisoner working. A sudden jolt of recognition coursed through him.

Brent was down there.

Jack immediately recognized his coworker's lanky frame, stooped over a shovel. He felt a stab of guilt as he saw Brent laboring away down there, guarded by a hulking man with a rifle. Brent shouldn't have been captured.

Jack once again regretted his mistake on the interstate. But there was no time for regrets. This was Jack's chance to make things right.

None of the other prisoners were guarded as closely as Brent. The other four prisoners worked at some distance from Brent, and only two guards watched over them. Brent must have done something they didn't like to be assigned his own babysitter. Jack couldn't help smiling at the thought.

Way to give them hell, Brent.

Jack looked over at the rest of the area. The lot was sandwiched between a bank and a fast food restaurant. A couple of other small businesses were to the north. Jack couldn't get a good view of what lay beyond the bank. He didn't like that. He didn't like not knowing who was just around the corner.

But it didn't matter. Less than ideal circumstances wouldn't change his course of action.

He knew what he had to do.

Jack ran down the stairs. Once back on the ground level, he made a quick exit through the side door. He emerged on the sun-drenched sidewalk just one block from the empty lot where Brent worked.

Edging along the exterior wall of the parking garage, he approached the fast food restaurant. He slipped around the building.

His heart pounded in his chest as he moved. Acid rose in his throat, burning his vocal cords. He wiped his sweaty palms on his pants.

He had to do this right.

Jack was so close to the work crew now. Stationing himself behind the concrete pillars of the drive-through, he watched and waited.

Four guards, at least in this lot. Who knew how many

other armed men were in the vicinity and would come running when they heard gunfire.

A wiry man holding a rifle paced along the fence closest to Jack. Two other guards were in the northern half of the lot. Brent worked on the far southern corner under the watchful eye of his massive guard.

Brent stood working in front of his guard, who stood behind him. That was a problem. Jack couldn't get a clean shot with Brent in front of the guy.

He would have to start firing at the other men. Hopefully, Brent would get out of the way long enough for Jack to take a shot.

Jack raised his rifle. He leveled it and peered through the scope.

"Hey! Who's that?"

The voice from one of the distant guards at the back broke Jack's concentration. Jack had been spotted.

Everything happened all at once.

The two distant guards to the north raised their rifles. Jack fired at the closest guard before he could lift his own weapon.

The second guard had begun to handcuff the prisoners. He snapped the cuffs shut over two prisoners before he raised his weapon at Jack.

The first guard fell. Before Jack could pivot toward the distant guards, they began shooting at him.

A bullet smashed into the concrete pillar. Jack ducked reflexively. Keeping himself lowered behind the pillar, he aimed at the first of the two distant guards.

The guard's aim was increasingly more accurate, but Jack kept firing. First one, then the other fell to the ground.

Jack looked over at Brent. The guard near him had begun firing toward Jack, but he was too far away. The guard started to run off to the side, both to take cover and to get closer to his target.

Just before the guard could get away, Brent lifted his shovel high and brought it down against the guard's head.

The guard's knees buckled underneath him, and he collapsed to the ground. Brent wrenched the rifle out of his hands and began running across the lot.

The two uncuffed prisoners scattered to the north, scaling the fence before they disappeared. The two prisoners who had been cuffed scrambled toward the fallen guards, searching for the keys to free their hands.

"Follow me!" Jack called to Brent. Jack took off running toward the parking garage again. He heard Brent following him several yards behind.

"Don't let them get away!" a guard shouted.

Voices were coming from the southwest corner of the lot. Jack pushed himself faster as he neared the parking garage.

Just before he ran inside the shelter of the garage, he glanced back. Brent was still behind him, closing the distance quickly.

The guard Brent had hit with a shovel had already recovered and was making his way across the lot at a brisk pace.

And three more armed men who had heard the gunfire were on their way, charging across the street and headed toward the parking garage.

15

Harvey's eyes met Charlotte's just as he was hit with the round from the .22.

He looked down at the hole in the side of his torso, then touched his fingers to the seeping blood.

His shock turned to fury as he looked back up at her. Charlotte aimed again, this time a little higher. She pulled the trigger.

The force of the second round knocked Harvey back to the ground. He lay there for several moments, blinking and staring up toward the sky.

Then, he was still.

Charlotte watched him, holding her breath.

Then she took a step forward. His chest had stopped rising and falling with his breath. His open eyes stared upward, unblinking.

She looked down at the gun. Then she walked to the car, where she placed it on the hood. She stood leaning against the vehicle, keeping her eyes on Harvey the whole time. She almost expected him to start moving again. But he never did.

After a while, she allowed herself to turn her back on the body nearby. She walked to the edge of the ditch, bent over, and vomited.

It was over.

Charlotte heard something from the road. She looked up to see a horse – with Annie riding it.

The horse was galloping at full speed, then came to a quick stop nearby on the road.

Annie sat there, staring with her mouth open – first at Harvey, then at Charlotte, then back to Harvey.

The horse switched its tail around at the flies landing on its body.

"I had to shoot him, Annie," Charlotte said, her voice shaky.

Annie nodded, her eyes still on the dead man in the ditch.

"He woke up. And he got his hands loose. And he was angry – so angry! He was about to get his feet free, too. If I had waited another second longer –"

Charlotte trailed off.

Annie looked at Charlotte sympathetically. "You did the right thing." She dismounted the horse clumsily and stood holding the reins. "Are you sure he's dead?"

Charlotte nodded, looking in the opposite direction of Harvey. She didn't like looking at him. "Pretty sure."

Annie led the horse closer to Harvey and nodded. "Yeah, he's dead." She looked over at her friend. "I'm sorry I had to leave you alone with him. But I'm proud of you, Charlotte. You defended yourself!"

Charlotte gave a weak smile. "I just don't want to make this a habit. Though, I do like that gun. I wouldn't mind having one of my own."

"We'll try to get you one," Annie said as she led the horse

around to the front of the car. "But for now, we don't have too much time to waste."

"Why? Did you steal that horse from someone, I'm guessing?" Charlotte asked.

"Kind of. I'm just borrowing her," Annie said as she handed the reins to Charlotte. "But I might have a meth head on my trail."

"Say what?" Charlotte asked, frowning. "And what am I supposed to do with this horse?" She looked up nervously at the animal.

"Just stay there for a second. If I can tie these ropes to the car..."

Charlotte watched as Annie struggled to tie the ropes around the Porsche's bumper.

"This is never gonna work," Charlotte said. "I've never heard of a horse pulling a car out of a ditch!"

Annie ignored her and kept working. Finally, she stood up, red-faced but smiling.

"Okay, girl," she cooed to the mare. "Come this way."

She led the horse by the reins downhill several feet.

"Charlotte, can you put the gear in neutral?" Annie asked. Charlotte grimaced from the pain as she moved, but she did as Annie asked.

Annie tied the ropes to the horse's harness as Charlotte came to stand beside her.

"You can do this," Annie said, looking into the mare's eyes.

Annie took the reins and clucked her tongue. The horse began to walk forward, but jolted when the ropes reached the end of their slack. Annie encouraged her forward, tugging on the reins. The horse pulled forward, bringing the ropes taut.

"That's it," Annie murmured. "Keep going."

Finally, the wheels on the Porsche began to roll forward. Then they stopped. The horse strained under the effort.

"You've got this," Annie said under her breath.

The horse kept straining, its muscles bulging under the effort. But finally, she got the wheels rolling again. Annie led the horse up toward the road, and the Porsche began to roll forward behind them.

Annie began to move backward at a brisk pace, leading the horse up and over the hill while the car rolled slowly behind. Just when the horse pulled the Porsche up to the road, Annie stopped her.

"Good girl!" she cooed to the horse, stroking its nose.

Charlotte made her way up to the road and stood looking at the Porsche, shaking her head.

Annie looked at her with raised eyebrows.

Charlotte threw her hands up. "You're right, you're right! I should know better than to doubt you, Mrs. Hawthorne!"

Annie smiled. "That's better. Now, I need you to put the car back in gear so it doesn't roll away. And put the emergency brake on."

Charlotte reached inside the car as Annie removed the ropes from the bumper and the horse's harness.

"Who's a good girl?" Annie said in a singsong voice as she ran her hand down the horse's back.

Charlotte walked around to the passenger's side of the Porsche and opened the door. "Yes, she's a very good horse. Now, can we get out of here?"

Annie frowned. "But what about her? Shouldn't I get her back to her home?"

Charlotte scoffed. "Didn't you say there was a lunatic down there? And that he was chasing you?"

Annie turned and looked down the road in the direction

of the house. "Yeah, I know it's not safe to go back down there. But I can't just leave this horse loose here."

"Do you really think a strung-out junkie is going to take good care of her?" Charlotte asked, leaning against the car.

"That's a very good point," Annie said. "And I think he killed the owner of the house – and the owner of this horse. I saw a dead man in the living room of the house. Then this younger guy ran out and attacked me..."

"He attacked you?" Charlotte asked, her eyes big. "And you're standing here talking to me instead of driving off? He could show up here with a weapon at any moment!"

Annie bit her lip. "You're right. I know you're right. But I just can't let this horse go. How will it survive alone out here?" She looked in the horse's big, dark eyes. "I wish we could take her with us."

"Maybe Jack could come back for the horse if he makes it to Loretta," Charlotte said. *"When* he makes it to Loretta, I mean."

Annie glanced at her friend.

"Shoot, I'm sorry, Annie," Charlotte said, cringing at her mistake. "I didn't mean anything by that, Annie. Really. Of course Jack is going to make it to Loretta. I'm sorry, it was a stupid mistake. I –"

Annie waved away her concern. "It's okay. I know you didn't mean anything by it."

But Annie knew Charlotte's slip of the tongue was probably closer to the truth. She had been denying it to herself the whole time, but deep down she knew it was true. As horrific as it might be to her, the chances were slim that Jack had survived a nuclear attack on Los Angeles.

After all, he had been downtown when their phone connection had been lost. Downtown Austin had been destroyed by a bomb, and Annie had been lucky to survive it. If downtown LA had been destroyed as well, what were the chances that Jack had gotten out in time?

The thought tore her apart, but she knew she would have to prepare herself for the possibility that she might never see her husband again.

And what about her family? All of their phones had been dead when she had tried to call them early Wednesday afternoon. Maybe the southeastern states had been obliterated, too. And Heather lived so close to Washington, DC. The attacks were probably the worst around the nation's capital.

Jack, Heather, Brody, Katie, Annie's parents... Maybe they were all gone.

Maybe Annie had lost everyone.

"Annie? Are you okay?" Charlotte asked. "You look like you saw a ghost."

Annie blinked a few times, then refocused on the horse. "I'm fine." She began to remove the harness.

"What I said was stupid," Charlotte said. "If anyone can survive this whole thing, it's Jack. I'm sure he's on his way home right now. He's just been delayed because... Well, because of everything. I guess you were right about what you were saying yesterday. It wasn't just Austin that was hit. It must've been the whole country. That's pretty clear now. But Jack got out of LA alive. I know he did."

"Yeah, I know," Annie said mildly. She swallowed the lump forming in her throat.

She patted the horse a few times. "Go back home," she whispered, looking into the horse's eyes. "If I can come back for you, I will."

Stepping aside, Annie gave the horse a final pat. She clucked her tongue. "Go home!"

The horse took off toward the house, as if it understood everything Annie had said.

Annie returned to the car and turned the key in the ignition. It started easily.

The two women drove off quickly in the Porsche. They soon passed the horse as it galloped to the west. Annie took one last look at the mare before they disappeared over the next hill.

She picked up speed. Her heart quickened as she drove. There was still one more challenge before they could get out of there.

Her palms grew sweaty as her hands clenched the steering wheel.

They were getting closer to the house where she had been attacked by a madman. She could still remember the sensation of being slammed against the ground.

Just one more hill, and they would come into view of that wooden house – and whatever was waiting for her nearby.

16

Suddenly, Heather came to a stop, skidding her feet on the ground to halt the bicycle. Frantically, she looked around.

Did she even know where she was?

She looked down at her feet. They were standing on a gravel road.

But when had she left the pavement?

She swallowed, fighting back another wave of nausea and fear. Somehow in her confusion and disorientation, she had taken a wrong turn.

Or had it been several wrong turns? Would she be able to find her way back to the highway at all?

She looked down at her shaking hands. They were covered in blood. *His* blood. And her arms and torso were soaked as well.

She turned her bike around and set out riding back the way she had come. Maybe she'd be able to retrace her steps.

A ways down the gravel road, she saw a sign for a National Forest campground. "Little Creek Campground," the sign read.

Feeling nauseous and disgusted from his blood on her body, she longed to wash the blood off herself. She turned down the road, hoping the creek would be flowing with water clean enough to rinse off.

Heather coasted into the campground and rode past the self-pay kiosk. A map on the information placard caught her eye, and she studied it, hoping to see a map of the general area. But she was out of luck – the map only detailed the tiny campground.

She rode past the campsites designated for tent camping. The campground was totally empty, which was at once eerie and comforting. She didn't want to see people, but the isolation was a little frightening. Had the EMP hit on a weekend, she figured, the campground would have been full of abandoned cars.

The sound of a bubbling creek beckoned her from the edge of the campground. Leaving her bike at the edge of the road, she approached the creek. Pines, firs, and spruce lined the sides of the little waterway. The tannins from the conifers' shed needles colored the transparent water a rich brown. It looked clean enough, so Heather began to wash herself in the freezing mountain water.

She removed her shirt and was about to wash the garment in the water, but she stopped herself.

Where was her backpack?

She cringed. It was gone. She must have left it behind in the town. In her confusion and panic, she hadn't even noticed it wasn't on her back.

Grumbling over her carelessness, she washed her skin as best she could, then put the soiled shirt back on. Her only other change of clothes was in her backpack, back in that small town. She didn't want to spend the night in a shirt splattered with blood, but it was better than a sopping wet shirt from the creek water.

Even if she knew how to get back there to the town, she wouldn't dare return to the scene of that terrible encounter.

And even worse – Heather had no food or drink with her.

She had at least consumed some juice and cookies back at the store, but the extras she had packed, along with her meager supply of dried fruit, were back in the town, still in her backpack.

Heather stood up and looked around. Somehow, she had managed to lose track not only of her whereabouts, but also of the time of day. The sun dipped low in the sky toward the horizon. It would be dark within minutes. There wasn't enough time to try to retrace her steps and return to the highway.

She would have to spend the night in the campground.

"No blankets, no clean clothes, no food, no drinking water," she said aloud, breaking the chatter of the birds flitting over the creek on their late afternoon tasks before night set in.

"You really screwed up," she said to herself. "And now you're talking to yourself."

I've probably lost my mind, she said, silently this time. Somehow, the thought of a mental breakdown was too real, too terrifying to utter aloud.

Grabbing her bike, she made her way uphill from the creek. She chose a campsite tucked away in the corner of the campground. She curled up in a cleared area underneath some white pines.

As the light faded, she closed her eyes. She wanted to sleep until first light, but she knew that was wishful thinking. The temperature was already dropping, and she knew it would be a chilly night without anything to ward off the cold.

I've got to find the highway again first thing in the morning.

Her stomach growled. Her thirst was so intense that she was tempted to go drink from the stream. But she knew a case of Giardia wouldn't help her situation.

She didn't open her eyes as darkness fell on the area, but she didn't fall asleep, either. Rustling noises in the bushes and forest nearby kept her on alert.

It's just animals. Go to sleep already.

But every time she dozed off, a noise from the forest startled her awake. And with each hour, she grew hungrier and weaker. As the night wore on, she began to shiver.

At some point, finding her way back to the highway in the morning no longer seemed to be her biggest challenge. She began to wonder if she was going to survive the night.

17

Paul Hawthorne stood on a bridge overlooking a reservoir.

The water was neon green from an algae overgrowth. Fish floated belly up on the surface. The air was thick with a putrid odor.

He kept walking.

Soon, he came upon a large complex for a chemical manufacturing company. Several large buildings were clustered behind a tall fence. The bad smell was stronger here.

He picked up his speed, anxious to leave the area. With the EMP having destroyed the electrical grid, he imagined the electric security measures of the chemical plant had failed. The toxic waste products had leaked into the reservoir.

He thought of the environmentalists who had always been causing trouble for the logging company he worked for. Tree huggers were always complaining about the trees his company harvested. They never seemed to listen to the company's statements about sustainable harvesting and their efforts to replant fast-growing tree species on the lands they held. One young guy had even chained himself to the highest branches of a tree on company grounds once, in protest of the logging company's operation.

Paul shook his head as he remembered it all.

The environmental groups had been wrong about Paul's employers. But maybe some of the critics had had a point about the operation of the chemical plants. At the very least, Paul figured the manufacturing company should have been more prepared for an electromagnetic pulse that would destroy the nation's power grid.

But then, *everyone* should have been more prepared.

And in the end, Paul thought, what did it matter? After all, he had lost his family. He had lost the only thing that mattered to him. And so many others, probably all over the country, had lost their lives or loved ones.

The world that he knew was over.

Now, he could only cling to the hope of seeing his brother again.

Paul moved quickly as he entered the edge of a small city. He was still in the Piney Woods of East Texas. Knowing he had a long journey ahead of him, he was preparing himself for several more days of walking toward his family's old ranch house in Loretta.

Paul tried to avoid walking through the centers of the populated areas he passed through. He didn't like how everyone seemed to stare at him in the towns.

He was far from the only person traveling on foot. Every populated area had people walking or on bicycles, forced to leave their cars behind. But his appearance made Paul stand out. His coworkers hadn't called him Paul Bunyan for nothing. At six feet seven inches, he towered over most people.

And now, he looked like he had been in an epic bar fight. His clothes were shredded in several places, and he was covered in bruises and scrapes from wandering around in the woods aimlessly for a couple of days. He knew he must look insane and dangerous, and he didn't want to frighten people.

But he couldn't avoid everyone. As he got farther into the town, he got more and more strange looks.

He had been to this town before with Marie and the children. They had passed through it about a year before. What was supposed to be a fun day trip to Houston had quickly turned into a tense argument with his wife over money. They had been discussing whether to buy a new car, trying to keep their voices down where the kids couldn't hear them over the radio blaring in the backseat of the minivan.

Marie insisted they needed to buy a new vehicle, one that was more up-to-date with safety measures for the kids. But Paul argued it was unnecessary and besides, they couldn't afford it.

The argument escalated until Brooklyn, their youngest, piped up.

"Mommy, don't you and Daddy love each other anymore?"

Their daughter's words stung. Both Paul and Marie assured the kids that they still loved each other, that it was just a disagreement. But Paul couldn't help feeling guilty. The conflict between him and his wife had intensified so much that the kids had started to worry.

Paul wished that he and Marie had stopped fighting that day, and the days after that. But they hadn't. The arguments continued, becoming more regular over the past year.

And Paul was ashamed to remember the times he had lost his temper and raised his voice at his own children. All the times he had been distant from them, annoyed at their antics. All the times he had wanted to be alone. He had taken out his frustration on his family.

Paul shook his head in sadness. How stupid he had been! If he had only known how quickly he would lose them, he would've never raised his voice at his wife or children. He would have relished every moment with them.

But there was nothing he could do to change the past. They were gone forever.

The sky darkened overhead from gathering clouds as he walked, matching Paul's mood.

He should have let Marie buy the damned car she wanted. He should have been better to her and the kids.

And most of all, he should have gotten them out of the house in time. He shouldn't have been working so far from home. They should never have bought a house so close to Dallas, a big city and a target for terrorism.

Paul had made so many mistakes.

He walked with his head down, avoiding the prying eyes of people on the street. He wanted to get out of this town fast, and return to the solitude of the open country.

A man's voice jostled him from his thoughts.

"Need a ride?"

Paul looked up and saw a guy in an old Jeep, the first running vehicle Paul had seen in days. The man had pulled over on the shoulder and was looking right at Paul, who had been so lost in his thoughts he hadn't even noticed.

"It's going to rain," the guy said. "Thought you could use a lift."

Paul shook his head. "No. I'm good."

The guy shrugged.

"Suit yourself," he said and took off again down the street.

Paul watched him disappear over the next hill. He didn't know why a stranger would be generous to him. In any case, he didn't want the ride. He didn't want to make small talk or act interested in what someone had to say.

He didn't trust anyone, either. He doubted he ever would again.

Except for Jack. His brother was about the only person left in the world he could trust.

Their dad had passed away ten years ago. Their mother had always been so close to her husband, and she began a steep decline after she lost him. A couple years later, she had passed away too.

Paul's grandparents were long gone. Aside from a few distant relatives scattered in Oklahoma and Arkansas, Paul and Jack had no living relatives. They only had each other.

Paul hoped that Jack could bury the hatchet and forget their old disagreements. They, too, had said things to each other Paul now regretted. But Jack was still his brother, and the only person he had left.

It started to rain lightly, but Paul kept walking. The rain didn't bother him. He liked it, even. It was cold and miserable, but Paul felt he deserved it. He wanted to be punished.

After two or three miles past the city limits, Paul came to a cornfield. It was getting dark, and Paul decided to turn in for the evening. He figured he had at least three more days to walk. When the rain let up, he ate the meager supply of food he had found in an empty house on the edge of town. He had considered sleeping in the old shack since it seemed to have been abandoned. But he didn't want to be comfortable. As long as he was haunted by the memory of his family, he couldn't afford himself comfort or shelter.

He lay down under a pine tree and closed his eyes. So much had already been lost. Could he really count on Jack and Annie still being alive? As he drifted off to sleep, he was plagued by the feeling that his brother was already dead.

18

Jack ran inside the garage and flung open the door to the stairwell.

"Hurry!" he urged Brent onward, holding the door open for him.

Brent ran through the door and began climbing the steps with Jack on his heels.

"Get off at the second floor," Jack said, keeping his voice low. He followed Brent through the door.

"Now what?" Brent asked, panting, as they stood on the next level, looking around.

"Shh," Jack whispered.

They listened as the sound of footsteps grew louder on the first floor. The guards were entering the garage.

Jack motioned Brent toward the row of cars before them. Moving lightly between the vehicles, the two men stationed themselves out of sight behind a large truck.

Jack drew his Glock from the holster, setting his rifle down silently on the floor. He needed to reload the rifle, but he didn't want to make a noise. The guards were running up the stairs now.

The stairwell door to the second floor flew open. Footsteps echoed through the dim garage. Another guard continued running up the stairs and emerged on the third floor. Jack heard him running on the ground overhead. Meanwhile, the guard on the second floor was getting closer.

Finally, Jack saw him. The man was moving slowly through the middle of the space, looking between each vehicle in both rows to the left and right.

The man was just three vehicles away now.

Jack raised the gun and waited for him to get closer.

The man took a few more steps forward, looking to the left and away from Jack and Brent.

It was Jack's only chance.

He pulled on the trigger. The man made an unexpected move to the left, and Jack missed.

The guy cursed. He ducked behind a vehicle and started firing in Jack's direction.

Damn!

Jack dodged his fire, adjusting his position behind the truck. He aimed again, waiting for the man to expose himself as he fired.

When the guy took aim again, Jack fired. This time, the guy was still, and Jack hit him.

He fell to the ground, gasping for breath. Jack saw his arm fall to the side with his pistol clanging to the ground.

Nearby, Brent blew out a jagged breath.

Jack brought his hand up, silently telling Brent to keep quiet.

Overhead, the guard was silent. Jack waited for his response, wondering what the guy was up to. The guard was waiting as well, considering his next move.

Jack stood up and silently began to make his way to the

fallen guard nearby. He picked up the man's gun and motioned for Brent to follow him to the other end of the parking garage. They crouched behind a minivan several yards from the scene of the shootout. Once in their new hiding place, they waited.

Upstairs, a truck engine started.

Brent looked at Jack with surprise. Jack got ready, waiting for the truck to appear.

The truck took off, peeling out overhead. It raced down the aisle of the third floor, then turned and began descending the ramp to the second floor. The driver took the next turn quickly and drove past the dead man lying on the floor.

The man steered the truck slightly to the left. He was heading straight for Jack and Brent. Somehow, he knew where they were hiding.

Jack opened fire on the driver. The shatterproof windshield cracked, but the bullets did not penetrate the glass. The truck kept charging ahead.

"Get out of here!" Jack shouted to Brent at his side. Brent, who had been watching the truck's advance in shock, finally came to his senses and crawled to the side.

Jack continued firing a second longer. When the truck was nearly upon him, he rolled to the side.

Unable to stop in time, the truck slammed into the wall. Jack watched the vehicle's front end crumple into the wall, destroying the engine. It was obvious that the truck wouldn't run again.

A sharp piece of metal splintered from the vehicle and sliced into Jack's lower leg as he rolled.

Jack came to a stop on his side, then raised his Glock once more, training his weapon on the driver. The engine smoked and hissed, blocking Jack's view of the cabin.

At last, the door slowly opened, and the driver emerged. He held a pistol in his hand and weakly tried to lift it.

Before the man could fire, Jack shot him twice in the chest. The man collapsed on the floor, his body slamming down just inches away from Jack.

Jack glanced at Brent, who was watching the scene from several feet away. The two men wordlessly pushed themselves to their feet and ran toward the stairwell.

In the stairwell, Jack struggled to make his injured leg work. Brent ran ahead, taking the steps two at a time to the third, and uppermost, floor.

"No," Brent said from the doorway to the third floor as he looked at at the top level. "There's nothing else up here. They must've had just that one truck stored on this level."

Gritting his teeth, Jack began the race down the stairs to the ground level.

"Wait," Brent said. "Shouldn't we see if any of the cars run on the second floor?"

"No," Jack said. "I already looked at them all. They're all too new to run. First floor as well. They just kept that one running vehicle on the top floor."

Brent followed Jack to the ground level. Jack entered the garage and turned to the right – away from the front entrance.

"Wrong way!" Brent said.

Jack kept going forward. "We're jumping out this back window."

Brent watched as Jack ran with a limp toward the big opening at the rear of the garage.

Jack gave a quick look outside the garage, then began to pull himself up and over the open window. He hit the ground with a jolt on his injured leg. Brent pulled himself over as well and jumped to the ground.

They ran along a row of junipers toward the apartment building a few yards from the parking garage. Jack looked over his shoulder. So far, no one was behind them.

Jack crossed to the east side of the building, and began to check the exterior doors of each apartment. Each of them was locked. He growled in frustration.

As Brent ran upstairs to search the second level's doors, Jack knew their time was running out. It wouldn't be long before more guards appeared and opened fire. Sooner or later, his luck was going to run out.

"This one's open," Brent said, leaning over the balcony and keeping his voice low.

Jack ran up the steps and followed Brent inside the apartment. The first order of business was checking every room of the apartment. Jack checked the two bedrooms while Brent looked through the kitchen and living room. Jack emerged from the bathroom after making sure it was clear, and raised his eyebrows at Brent in a question.

"All clear out here," Brent said as he turned to look out the front window. "And so far, I don't see anyone out there coming for us." He bolted the front door and followed Jack to the rear bedroom.

The men peered through the window and watched as a small group of male and female guards ran down the street behind the apartment building and toward the abandoned lot where Brent had worked. Jack reloaded his Glock, keeping an eye on the people below. He didn't know where they were headed or if they had seen him and Brent run inside the apartment.

"That was crazy back there!" Brent said. "You just started picking off guys out there at the work site. And how did you know where to find me? And – how did you get out of C Block?"

Brent looked at Jack, eager for answers. Jack finally glanced at him.

"I'll tell you later."

Brent sighed and looked out the window.

Jack inspected the rifle Brent had lifted from his guard. Jack didn't have any more ammo for the weapon, and it was low. Jack set the rifle down and watched as the group dispersed at the end of the block. Several went to check on the fallen men in the work site. A few turned toward the parking garage.

"We may not have much time," Jack said. "But we can't make a run for it now. They're too close. They'd see us running out of here. We'll have to wait."

"Wait for what?" Brent asked, staring out at the people moving over the abandoned lot. "For them to find us?"

"Or for them to move past us," Jack said.

"Are we going to go get Naomi?" Brent asked.

"Of course."

Brent sighed, relieved. He watched as Jack removed the rifle he carried over his left shoulder and held it in front of him.

"I know you've had next to zero training with guns," Jack said. "But I have no choice but to let you use this. I need some backup."

Brent nodded and reached for the rifle.

"Not just yet," Jack said. "Keep it pointed away from non-targets. Remember, never point it at anything you're not prepared to kill. Always be sure of your target and what's behind it."

Jack handed it to him carefully. "And keep your finger off the trigger and outside the guard until you're ready to shoot. These things are powerful, so brace yourself when you shoot it."

Jack showed him how to hold the rifle and position his body for maximum stability and accuracy. Brent paid close attention and did as he was instructed.

Jack sighed as Brent held the rifle, feeling his way into a good stance while aiming the gun out the window. "You really need more target practice than what we did the other day."

"Desperate times call for desperate measures," Brent quipped, studying the area outside.

Jack crossed through the rooms to look out the front window.

"I don't see them out here," Jack said. "They're probably searching the parking garage right now."

Brent returned to stand by Jack's side. "You sure we shouldn't make a run for it now?"

"Not yet," Jack said. "They're really close out there. And besides, I need some information from you."

"Like what?"

"I need to know everything you know about the layout of this place," Jack said, never taking his eyes away from the window.

Brent shrugged. "I don't know much. I just know the interstate is that way, to the north. They took us all down to their headquarters that day, and from there they took me farther from the interstate and over this way, to the right."

Jack nodded. "Right, we're about five blocks west of the headquarters and six or seven south of the interstate. Where do they have you sleeping?"

"In this big dorm building for the college students."

"Where's the college campus?"

"The dorm is about five to eight blocks that way," Brent said, pointing.

"Southwest," Jack supplied.

"Right. And the main campus buildings are farther south from the dorms, I guess. They haven't taken us that way."

"And what's between here and there?" Jack asked.

Brent shrugged. "A lot of little shops. Restaurants, bookstores, coffee shops. Some apartment buildings like this one."

"Did you see where they took Naomi?"

Brent shook his head. "No. They split us all up that day as soon as they took us out of the headquarters. All I could see was that they were taking Naomi straight south. And they took you and me off to the west and east."

Jack nodded. "And they could have taken her off in some other direction after that first block, too. They intentionally did it that way so we wouldn't know where the others were."

"Yeah. They're pretty slick that way."

"What about the cars they steal? Do you know where they keep them?"

Brent shook his head again. "No, not really. I haven't seen the Pathfinder since they stole it from us the other day. Sometimes I see them driving other cars and trucks through the streets, usually hauling stuff around. But I don't know where they keep them."

Jack sighed. "No idea?"

Brent thought about it a bit more. "Not for sure, no. But if I had to guess, I'd place my bets on Naomi being to the southeast of here, and the cars being at some point south of that."

"Except for a stray vehicle they have tucked away here and there," Jack added. "Like the truck at the top of that garage."

"That's now crashed to pieces on the second floor," Brent said sadly. "I wish we could have gotten that truck!"

Jack didn't answer, but he brought his finger to his lips, then pointed out the window toward the garage. Voices from the garage made their way to the window where Jack and Brent waited.

The two men lowered themselves further at the window to keep from being spotted.

"Are you ready?" Jack asked.

"For what?" Brent asked under his breath.

"For anything," Jack mumbled.

Brent didn't answer. He could only stare, transfixed, as a guard ran from the parking garage toward the apartment building where they now waited.

19

Brody moved through the woods quickly. It wasn't dark yet on the road, but here in the woods the light was already gone. He wanted to cover as much ground as possible before he flicked the flashlight on.

Batteries, along with everything else, were in short supply.

He occasionally tied little bits of cloth, torn from a rag, to the branches. Not only to find his way back to the road, but also to mark the area he had searched. He has hoping to find his dad tonight, but in case he didn't, he didn't want to waste time searching the same area tomorrow.

His sudden improvement in health was remarkable. He had woken up that day feeling a bit better, and had improved each hour of the day. Now he felt like he'd never been sick. He didn't know what to think about it. Could he really have gotten over the radiation sickness? He was afraid of what the answer might be, so he had tried not to think about, instead choosing to busy himself with productive tasks.

Still, though, he couldn't help feeling hopeful. Less than

twenty-four hours before, he had been resigned to die. He had been torturing himself with guilt over going outside that day and getting exposed to the nuclear fallout. What would Katie do without him? She had already lost one parent. Fifteen, almost sixteen, was too young to lose both one's parents.

And Katie might never forgive him – or worse, she might never forgive herself for her anger at her father for leaving her too soon. When she got older and could look back, she would realize that her anger had been misplaced. Brody didn't want his Katie's last memories of her father be tainted with mixed-up, toxic emotions.

Brody sighed as he moved through the thick underbrush. He had already searched on the other side of the road. He was beginning to lose hope.

In the area immediately surrounding his father's truck, there had been no sign of a struggle. The forest had looked undisturbed. And anyway, it didn't really make sense that his father would have left the safety of his vehicle and gone off in the woods if he were injured.

Brody flicked on the flashlight and turned around, heading again toward the road.

He made his way out to the road and began to pedal his bike back home. He would have to tell his mother and Katie the truth.

He believed his father had been abducted.

20

Jack and Brent watched a guard run toward the apartment complex. Just before he got to Building B, where Jack and Brent hid, the guard turned to the left and veered toward Building A.

"Now's our chance," Jack said. "While he's busy with the other building, we'll run out of here toward the south."

Only one guard had been sent to check the apartment complex. It was a lucky break for Jack, who had been counting on several men scouring the buildings and rooting out their hiding place. As long as they were quick and didn't make too much noise, he hoped they could escape undetected.

He quietly opened the door. Carrying the rifle, Brent followed him through the entrance, and they darted across the outdoor balcony that ran along the building's facade. At the end, they ran down the steps. Jack heard the doors in the building nearby being opened and shut as the guard made his way through the apartment units.

Brent followed Jack past two more buildings, then they came to a fence. Behind them, the guard was making his way to the second building. They only had a few moments. Scaling the chain-link fence, they took off running behind a row of businesses on the other side. A pit bull tied up in the backyard of a house across the street started barking.

"Damn!" Brent muttered. "That dog's gonna give us away."

"Run faster," Jack said over his shoulder as he took off sprinting toward a cluster of houses on the next block.

They scaled another low fence and landed in the backyard of a small house. They stopped to catch their breath and listen for any signs of someone following them.

It was quiet, but Jack didn't dare speak and alert anyone of their presence. He gestured silently to Brent: they'd keep moving through the backyards of the residential street until they got to a large hotel he'd spotted to the south. Brent nodded his understanding, and they pressed on.

The two men kept to the shadows as much as they could, seeking shelter behind trees and vehicles whenever possible. Each new temporary patch of cover they arrived at, they would stop, look, and listen for people nearby.

Under the cover of a tall pine in one backyard, they suddenly heard voices from inside the house nearby. Rather than risk a confrontation, Jack took off running.

They tore through several more backyards, scaling the low fences that separated some of them. Jack's heart pounded in his chest. His lungs screamed, his injured leg protested, urging him to stop.

But he couldn't, not yet.

Keep running.

At the end of the block, they could finally rest. Jack led Brent through an opening in the wooden fence and emerged in a back alley. They crouched between two vehicles parked at the end of the alley.

Catching their breath, they scanned the surroundings, narrowing in on the hotel across the street.

"That must be where she is!" Brent whispered. "Those are all female prisoners."

Jack watched as groups of women were being marched from the south along the sidewalk of the street adjacent to them, some one hundred and twenty yards away. One by one, the groups were led to the parking lot of the hotel. Each group was supervised and directed by a female guard or two. Most of the women had plastic ties around their wrists to prevent any kind of rebellion. The women looked exhausted and broken, both physically and mentally. They walked with their eyes down, cringing whenever a guard spoke or drew near. They were sunburned and covered in dirt. They had clearly been doing hard labor.

Jack felt a jolt of panic when he saw the women. Naomi had already been so closing to giving up days ago. How would she respond to the brutal treatment of these people – these *slavers* – now?

The guards made the women all line up and wait to be counted. Satisfied that they had all the prisoners, the guards led the women inside the hotel, one small group at a time.

"It's lunchtime," Brent whispered. "They did the same thing with us. Handcuffed us and brought us inside to our rooms to eat some disgusting slop."

As the guards brought each group of women around to the front entrance, Jack and Brent could get a closer look at them. Group by group, the two men waited in anticipation, hoping to see Naomi's face among the women. When the last group was brought inside, Jack sighed in disappointment. Naomi wasn't being kept prisoner here.

Brent glanced at Jack. "Should we keep going? Maybe they have another women's prison closer to the campus."

Jack nodded. "Yeah, we should keep heading south," Jack said in the faintest of whispers. "Then we can cut over to the east and move up north to look on the other roads."

"Sounds good."

"But the problem is this area is thick with guards," Jack said. "It's going to be harder than ever not to be seen moving around here."

Brent looked around. "If we could cross this street, we'd be in better shape. All those trees on the sidewalk over there would give us cover. Plus, there's another alley behind that block to the west. Might be safer."

Jack followed with his eyes the route Brent was describing. It would be difficult to cross the street, but Brent was right – if they could pull it off, the alley would be a much better option than the main road. He waited as a small troop of young teens pulling bicycle trailers passed. Once they were out of sight, the street was relatively empty. All the female prison guards were inside the hotel.

"*We'll* be guards," Jack muttered.

"What?"

"We'll cross the street like we're supposed to be here. Like we're guards," Jack said.

Brent frowned, looking doubtful. "I guess. I mean, if you think that'll work."

Jack gave one last look up and down the street, then stood up from the car he crouched behind. He adjusted the rifles, then emerged from the alley and walked out onto the side street. Turning right, he moved down the sidewalk toward the main intersection. Brent followed his lead.

At the intersection, Jack stepped off the sidewalk casually into the street. He began to stride across the street confidently, with Brent beside him.

The plan wouldn't work if they ran into any guards up

close – the gang's members had probably all been briefed on the fugitives' physical descriptions and would be looking for Jack and Brent. But maybe the men's cool, unworried demeanor would fool anyone watching from a distance.

In any case, a guard watching two men scurry across the street in a panic would definitely know something was amiss.

And so Jack sauntered across the street, looking up and down the block calmly as if patrolling the area.

Jack's pulse pounded in his temples. He fought the urge to break into a run. He wanted desperately to escape the area and hide out of sight of any guards watching from the hotel windows or from down the street. But he restrained himself, forcing his legs to carry him even slower than he thought necessary. A real guard on patrol duty wouldn't be in a hurry.

At the end of the intersection, they headed toward the alley on the next block. Beside him, Brent let out a tense exhale once they turned into the alley.

"That was awful," Brent whispered. "I thought for sure we'd be caught out in the open like that."

"Keep your voice down," Jack breathed. "We're not out of the woods yet."

The two passed through the alley at a brisk pace, constantly on the lookout for anyone who might be following. At the end of the block, they looked around. There were only smaller homes on the surrounding blocks, so they crossed the next, smaller street. The alley continued on the next block.

Jack's leg was still hurting from the metal scrap from the truck, but he was more concerned with the increasing difficulty in finding Naomi. The gang's territory was even larger than he had suspected, and it was going to be hard to find her. And the more time they spent searching up and down the streets, the more likely a run-in would be.

The alley bisected the block, running between the two rows of homes. Many of the homes had small storage sheds or detached garages abutting the alley.

Jack glanced at a shed up ahead to the right, then at the garage in the adjacent yard.

Jack approached the far edge of the shed. A sudden flash of movement to the right caught his eye.

But before he could react, a man hiding behind the shed lunged out at him.

Jack felt a sharp, sudden pain in his thigh. He groaned as a fiery sensation flared through his leg.

He looked down to see the man withdraw a fixed blade knife from his outer thigh.

Before Jack knew what was happening, Brent made a sharp movement. Lifting the butt of his rifle up, Brent brought the weapon down across the man's head.

The man fell over on the ground. Brent hit him again on his head.

Brent took a step back and looked at the man, who was bleeding from his head. His eyes wide and bulging, he shuddered on the ground. Brent stared at him, frozen in place.

Jack grabbed his arm and pulled. "We've got to get out of here."

Snapping out of his reverie, Brent blinked and took off behind Jack. The two men ran through the alley. Jack's attacker wouldn't be coming after them anytime soon – he was probably unconscious, Jack figured. But the noise of the confrontation might alert any guards in the area to Jack's and Brent's whereabouts.

They had to get far away, fast.

Jack's head was pounding as they ran toward the end of

the block. They emerged from the shade of the trees lining the alley. The sunlight hit his face, blinding him momentarily as he drew closer to the intersection.

His leg was bleeding fast. With each breath, he felt more lightheaded. As he ran out from the cover of the alley and began to cross the side street, he began to feel woozy.

His vision was fragmenting. Splintered images swirled around in front of his eyes.

He didn't have much time.

21

Heather shivered in the night cold. It had been a few hours since she had lain down and shut her eyes at the campsite. She would have to accept the inevitable. She would get no sleep that night. Fear, hunger and thirst kept her wide awake.

Rising to her feet, she got on her bike and pushed off. She was growing hungrier as the night wore on, and she didn't want to get too weak to make it home.

A waning gibbous moon had finally risen about a half hour ago. Now, it cast a silvery light on the gravel road. She rode out of the campground road and turned on the gravel street where she had first realized she was lost. With some luck, she hoped she would be able to make it back to the highway. She had to try. Staying any longer at the campsite would surely mean death.

———

Riding the bike helped to warm her up, but it made the gnawing hunger in her belly worse.

Around the first light of the morning, Heather made it to a crossroads. She came to a stop and stared at her options. The road she was on ended, and she could turn left or right on a gravel road.

With the light of the rising sun, she could at least orient herself to the directions. But maybe she had taken so many turns in her confusion yesterday that she couldn't assume that west would take her to the highway.

Finally, as the sun illuminated the land, she spotted a windmill down the road to her left. She remembered passing that windmill. She grinned as she pedaled off to the left. Soon, she hoped to make it to the highway.

It was late morning when she finally made it to her parents' house, having found her way back to the highway soon after sunrise. When she at last saw the long, uphill driveway, she felt a surge of energy and she pushed the bicycle faster toward her family home.

She could scarcely contain her excitement. Finally, this nightmare would come to an end. Her mother and father would be there. And they would make everything okay.

Finding the door was locked, she knocked loudly and impatiently. Taking a moment to look around, she noticed her mom's vehicle was parked out front, but her father's truck wasn't there. That wasn't too surprising – he had probably been driving somewhere when all the cars stopped working. And then he had walked home.

She could scarcely wait to see her family.

The front door finally opened. Heather was overcome with joy to see her mother standing before her.

"Heather! My baby!" her mother exclaimed. She opened

her arms wide, pulling her daughter in close. "You made it all this way! But you look awful! Are you all right?"

Heather nodded against her mother's shoulder. "I'm fine now. Everything's fine now that I'm home."

Myra looked off the porch to see Heather's bike on the ground. "Goodness! Did you ride your bike all the way from Roanoke? You must be exhausted!"

She led her daughter inside, closing the door behind her.

"You come sit down here," Myra said, taking Heather by the hand and plopping her down at the dining table. "What do you need? You must be starving!"

Heather nodded. "I need water most of all."

Myra poured her a glass of water and brought it to Heather, who downed the glass instantly. Myra poured her another glass.

"I'll get you some food," Myra said as she left the water pitcher for her daughter and hurried into the kitchen.

"Heather?"

Heather looked up to see her niece on the stairs.

"Katie!"

Katie ran to give her aunt a hug. Surprised, Heather stood up and wrapped her arms around the teenager, who looked up at her aunt with a grin.

"It's so good to see you, kiddo! And you're almost taller than me now! But *why* are you here?" Heather asked, collapsing back on the couch and downing the second glass of water. "You didn't come by yourself, did you?"

"No. Dad wanted to come here," Katie said.

"Oh, Brody's here?" Heather asked, glancing up at her mother.

"Yeah, he's still sleeping," Katie said.

"Lazy bones," Heather said, grinning. She was elated to

be back home. And better yet, her brother and niece were there, too. Things were looking up.

She grabbed a handful of chocolate raisins from a package on the table. "When did you get here, Katie?"

"Two nights ago," Katie said. "We rode our bikes here. It took all day."

"And that was just thirty miles," Myra said from the kitchen. "How long did it take you to come from Roanoke?"

"This is my third day riding," Heather said. "I waited two days to leave – after . . . after the bomb hit Roanoke."

Myra looked up. "Roanoke, too?" She stood bracing the counter as if she had suddenly felt dizzy. "Thank God you're okay!"

Heather nodded. "Yep. A coworker warned me at work that day, so I got out in time. He had some kind of tip from a friend at the Capitol. If I hadn't listened to him, I probably wouldn't be alive."

Myra shook her head and returned to the table with a plate of food. She threw her arms around her daughter again, who had already begun to tear into the food. "I'm just so glad you made it. I haven't been able to think about anything but you and your sister and –"

Myra stopped herself, then continued quickly. "I'm just so glad you came home, where you ought to be. I never want to let you out of my sight again!"

Heather swallowed a large mouthful of chicken and looked around. "Where's Dad?"

Myra and Katie looked at each other. Then Myra looked away.

"Mom?" Heather asked, her voice becoming higher-pitched. "Where's Dad?"

"Well, you know, he went to the hardware store that day.

Wednesday. And then, all the lights went out and the cars stopped. I –"

Heather pushed her chair from the table and began to walk toward the back porch.

"Dad?" she called. "Dad!"

"Heather, sweetie," Myra began, her face lined with worry. "We've been looking for him for days. I just don't know what to do anymore."

Heather kept moving through the house, opening all the doors as if she'd find her father hiding. She had stopped listening to her mother. She couldn't bear to hear it.

"Heather, please sit down," Myra said. "I have to talk to you."

But Heather was already running up the stairs.

"Dad! Dad, where are you?"

Heather ran into her parents' bedroom. Empty. Then she charged into the spare rooms. She first looked in her old bedroom, then Annie's, which was now being used by Katie. She let out a frustrated cry as the realization sunk in that her father was actually gone. She didn't know where he was or how he'd disappeared, but just that her father was gone.

Angered and panicked, she charged into Brody's room, fully prepared to demand answers from her big brother about their missing father.

But she froze when her eyes fell on Brody. He lay in bed, his eyes closed, and his skin an odd color.

He looked terribly ill.

22

Annie drove the Porsche over the final hill, then began to charge down the highway.

The house came into view.

"Is that where the meth head lives?" Charlotte asked, looking off to the right.

"It's where he lives now," Annie said. "I think he murdered the owners of the house."

Charlotte craned her neck to look down the driveway as they got closer.

"Oh, I see him!" Charlotte said, recoiling.

Annie looked over toward the driveway. She saw the man who had attacked her earlier. Hearing the approaching vehicle on the highway must have provoked him to take action. He was running at full throttle toward the highway.

But he was too late. The Porsche passed the turnoff toward the house before he could get close. For a moment, Annie braced herself, worried that the man might start firing a gun at them. But they passed the area without incident. She returned her eyes to the road, determined not to miss any more obstacles on the highway. She wanted to get to Loretta without any more problems.

Charlotte sighed in the passenger seat. "I'm glad he didn't have a gun! He looked crazy."

Annie nodded silently beside her. She felt her racing heart began to slow down. They had escaped one more madman. She took a few deep breaths as she drove the Porsche around a tight curve.

"Do you think we'll be there in an hour?" Charlotte asked hopefully. "I can't wait to lie down in a bed. Finally."

"About an hour and a half," Annie said. "And I have a quick stop to make before we get to the ranch."

Charlotte looked at her, somewhat alarmed. "A stop? Where?"

"I just want to stop and check on a neighbor in Loretta," Annie said. "She's an old friend of the family. Jack and I always stop and make sure she's all right. She's elderly and all alone. It won't take long, though. Loretta is a tiny town. And Jack's ranch is two or three miles on the other side of town."

"Okay," Charlotte said as she settled in her seat, trying to find a comfortable position despite her injuries. "As long as no one starts shooting at us or tries to steal the car."

Annie laughed. "I don't think that would happen in Loretta. It's a friendly little town. But you're right, we have to be careful just the same."

Annie gripped the steering wheel with both hands as she drove through the peaceful countryside. She could hardly believe how good it felt to be on the move at high speeds again. They had been so vulnerable, stuck on the side of the road for the past thirty-six hours. Now, they had mobility, and that meant power and freedom. Annie promised herself that she'd fight with everything she had to keep access to the car.

She felt the tension in her shoulders ease up.

Almost there. Soon, they would be safe.

Finally, the first house on the eastern edge of Loretta appeared. Annie felt excitement building in her chest. They had almost arrived.

The Porsche's deceleration woke Charlotte from her nap.

"Where are we?" she asked groggily.

"Almost to Loretta," Annie said. "And I'm gonna make my stop first right here."

Annie turned in a short driveway on the outskirts of town and parked the car in front of a modest single-story home. A cheery flower garden out front was well cared for and made the property colorful.

"This is Edith's house," Annie said as she killed the engine.

Annie got out of the car, stretching her arms overhead to get the kinks out from the drive.

"You wait here," she told Charlotte. "I'll be right back."

Charlotte watched as Annie walked past a ten-year-old Ford sedan parked in the driveway. Annie climbed the steps to the porch, then knocked loudly on the front door.

Inside the car, Charlotte struggled to turn around without pulling too much at her wounds. She wanted to keep an eye on the highway. Loretta looked like a sleepy little town, but Charlotte didn't trust anyone anymore. What if one of the neighbors had heard the Porsche and took a notion to stealing it?

Annie knocked a second time on the front door, louder this time. When there was again no answer, she pressed her face against the glass of the front window, shielding her vision from the sun. After a moment, she came down from the porch and began to circle around toward the back door.

"I don't hear anything inside," Annie said to Charlotte as she passed. "It's weird. She should be at home."

Charlotte waited in the car as Annie was gone for several minutes. Charlotte wished her friend would hurry. She didn't like being left in the car alone. She picked up the gun from its resting place on the middle console and put it in her lap, running her finger along the cool metal of the barrel. Having the gun there made her feel a little less afraid.

Finally, Annie reappeared and returned to the car. She didn't say anything, but Charlotte could see the worry on her face.

"What is it?"

"She's not here," Annie said as she started the Porsche. "I let myself in with a key she keeps hidden in the backyard. It looks like she hasn't been around for a couple of days."

"Maybe she's staying with family now," Charlotte said. She was relieved when Annie started to back the car out of the driveway. Charlotte was anxious to get to Jack's house. She hoped that they could feel at least a little safer there.

Annie shook her head. "She doesn't have any family left."

"Friends in town?" Charlotte suggested. "Maybe they didn't want an elderly woman living on her own after the attacks."

"Maybe, though Edith didn't have a lot of close friends in this town. She moved here kind of late in life. That's why Jack and I always checked on her. But you're right – she could be staying with someone nearby," Annie said with an uneasy edge to her voice, despite her words of agreement.

"Yeah, or she's just visiting someone in town for the day," Charlotte said dismissively. "I'm sure she's fine."

Annie nodded. "Yeah, you're right. She probably just wanted some company."

She bit her lip as she pulled the Porsche onto the highway and drove on toward the center of town.

"You're still worried," Charlotte observed.

"I don't know, Edith's empty house just doesn't sit right with me," Annie said. "It *feels* like something is wrong."

Charlotte raised her eyebrows in an exaggerated way. "You think someone *murdered* her?" she asked in a mock panic.

Annie rolled her eyes. "I know it sounds silly. But Edith's always at home when we come through here. It's just weird."

Charlotte shook her head. "You worry way too much, Annie."

Annie didn't answer. The sensation that something was wrong nagged at her, but she continued on as they began to enter the center of town.

"So this is Loretta proper?" Charlotte asked.

Annie nodded. "This is it. Population 685."

Charlotte whistled. "That *is* tiny!"

The highway ran through the center of the tidy, quiet little town. A couple dozen houses stood on the main road, with several more on the blocks running north and south of town.

"Is this all?" Charlotte asked incredulously as they reached the middle of the settlement.

"This is pretty much it," Annie said. "Isn't it great?"

"If you say so," Charlotte muttered. She was beginning to miss Austin. *Old* Austin – before the attacks.

Charlotte watched as they passed a tiny community center, a little restaurant, and a well-maintained church. All the civic buildings were closed up. There wasn't a light on in the town, nor the sound of a motor running. Clearly, the EMP had hit here, too.

Charlotte glanced at Annie, who was chewing on her lip again. "*Now* what's wrong?"

"No one's outside," Annie said, glancing up and down the streets. "Usually you see at least a few people outside, working in their gardens or whatever. And with the EMP, you'd think there'd be more people outside. It's not like they're all indoors watching TV."

Charlotte shrugged. "They're probably freaked out and want to stay indoors. Especially when some out-of-towners in a fancy sports car roll into town."

"Yeah, that's true," Annie said distractedly. She looked up and down all the side streets as they traversed the little town. Not a soul was out on the street, or standing in a yard or on a porch.

She shivered, suddenly feeling a chill run down her spine.

Why was the town of Loretta empty? It felt like a ghost town.

And the fact that Edith wasn't at home made Annie even more on edge.

Something felt wrong. Annie didn't know what it was, but fear began to take her over. As she floored the gas pedal and left the empty town behind, one thought repeated over and over in her mind.

What if something's wrong at the Hawthorne house?

23

"Brody?"

Heather stood in the doorway of the bedroom, watching her brother.

He lay in bed motionless, his eyes closed. His skin had an ashen pallor. Seeing her brother like that struck fear in Heather's heart.

What had happened to Brody?

Finally, his eyes slowly opened. It took him a long time to focus on Heather. She slowly walked inside the room and stood at his bedside.

"Heather, is that you?" he asked in a weak voice.

Heather swallowed. "Yes, it's me. Brody, what happened to you?"

He blinked a few times. His eyes moved from Heather to the doorway.

"Oh, dear God," Myra gasped.

Heather spun around to see her mother standing in the door. Katie appeared behind her a moment later, her face filling with shock and surprise.

"What happened to him?" Heather demanded.

Myra entered the room, staring at her son. She opened her mouth several times as if to speak, but her voice eluded her.

Anger and frustration welled up inside Heather's chest. "What's going on here?" she asked, looking back at Brody.

"The bomb," Brody muttered.

Heather looked helplessly from Brody to her mother, then back to Katie, who stood with her mouth open in the doorway.

"He was supposed to be getting better," Katie said angrily.

Myra wiped tears from her face as she took Brody's hand.

"He's so cold," Myra said. She pulled the covers up under his chin.

Brody waved her away. "It's radiation exposure," he told Heather. "I was too close . . . to Ground Zero when the bomb went off."

"What?" Heather asked incredulously, staring at him.

"He was downtown in Johnson City," Myra said sadly. "He was sick when he got here two days ago, but he was doing so much better yesterday. He thought it might have just been the flu. We thought he was going to get better," she with a shaking voice, looking back at Katie.

Katie stood in place as she stared at her father. She was stricken.

"What is this?" Heather asked. She grabbed something off the nightstand and held it in her palm, staring at a small, blackened object.

"It's a tooth!" Myra exclaimed.

Heather stared at the tooth in disbelief. "Why is it black?"

Myra shook her head sadly. "It must be from the radiation. It's poisoning him from the inside."

Brody took a breath. "It fell out sometime this morning."

He opened his mouth and pulled his lips back to show his teeth.

Heather looked closely. Several of his teeth were turning various shades of gray and black. She recoiled in terror and disgust and returned the tooth to the nightstand.

She ran a hand through her hair nervously and took a few steps back.

"How can this be happening?" she asked.

No one answered. Myra stood in place, looking at Brody.

Heather began to pace back and forth across the room.

"What do we do?" she asked frantically.

"I don't know," Myra answered. Her face twisted in anguish.

"There's got to be something we can do!" Heather snapped. The powerlessness and frustration of the situation were beginning to overwhelm her.

"Katie?" Brody asked. "Where's Katie?"

Heather and Myra turned toward the door. Katie was gone.

Myra sniffed and wiped her tears. "I'll go look for her."

Myra left the room. Heather could hear her calling Katie's name as she walked down the steps.

Heather returned to Brody's side and took a deep breath. "What can I do, Brody? Isn't there anything I can do to help?"

Brody shook his head. "I'm sorry you have to see this," he said slowly. "Nothing can be done."

Heather swallowed the lump in her throat and looked around the room. "What about Dad? Where is he? No one's telling me anything!"

Brody closed his eyes. "He's missing. Been gone four days. His truck is abandoned on a dirt road a few miles from here."

Heather's face distorted in pain. Her world was falling apart right before her eyes.

They were quiet, listening to their mother moving through the rooms downstairs calling for Katie. The screen door opened and shut, and Myra's calls grew faint as she walked down the porch steps and into the front yard.

Katie had run off somewhere, but that fact barely registered in Heather's mind. Her brother was gravely ill, and her father was out there somewhere. Missing!

Heather took a step away. "I've got to go look for him! Why is no one looking for him? This is crazy. I – I don't understand what's going on around here!"

"We looked, Heather," Brody said hoarsely. "We all have. You should keep looking for him, but –"

Heather spun around toward the door and began to charge out of the room, too impatient to listen to what Brody had to say. She had to take action now!

"Wait," Brody requested.

Heather looked back at him, almost cringing from the sight of her brother in such a weakened state.

"What is it?" she asked, blinking back tears.

"Don't go. Stay here with me," he said. "Please."

Heather unclenched her fists and let go of the doorknob. She took a deep breath, then slowly dragged a chair over to the side of his bed. She put aside her frantic need to search for her father, to go tearing through the woods on a wild quest to find him, going out of her mind with worry and frenzied panic. She exhaled deeply and sat beside her brother, taking his cold hand in her own.

"I'm here," she said.

24

"Hey, are you all right?" Brent asked while keeping pace with Jack as they ran through the alley. Brent was out of breath and spoke between gasps of air.

Jack was getting dizzy, but he pushed himself on. "That shed up there," he said, indicating a small storage shed in the alley. They had crossed the street and were entering the next block.

Brent turned the handle on the shed door and ducked inside. Some light streamed in a tiny window on one wall, and he looked around. It was empty.

"All clear," he said and watched as Jack followed him inside, limping on both legs now.

Jack's pants leg was saturated with blood. He fought the dizziness threatening to take him over, and looked around the shed for anything he could use to stop the bleeding. Brent helped him look, too, but finally Jack gave up and took his shirt off. He applied pressure to the wound, causing his eyes to smart from the pain.

The shed was filled with assorted junk – old lawn

mowers, broken-down electronics, and furniture in ill repair. Jack picked out a chair from the corner jumble and sat down.

Brent saw the blood flowing from Jack's leg and gasped.

"Man, he got you good," Brent said, seeing how badly Jack had been stabbed.

Behind him, Brent dug through the piles of junk. "I doubt I'm going to find a first aid kit in here," he said. "But it would sure be a stroke of luck if I could."

Brent looked down at Jack, who was breathing in short gasps.

"Here, put your feet up," Brent said as he dragged a table across the floor and helped Jack elevate his legs. "Isn't that what you're supposed to do if you're in shock?"

Jack didn't answer, but he put his feet up. Brent took the shirt from him and began to apply pressure to the wound. His eyes moved over the walls, landing on a stack of boxes nearby.

"If I could just find some alcohol swabs. A bottle of peroxide. Something." He spoke under his breath, more to himself than to Jack.

"And we're going to need some bandages, too," Brent continued. Jack's silence was making him nervous, and he was eager to fill the empty room with his words. "You probably need stitches. I wish my mom was here. She'd know what to do. She's a nurse."

Jack tipped his head back and closed his eyes.

"You don't look so good, Jack."

Jack opened his eyes again and gazed in Brent's direction clumsily, as if his vision were fading. "I'm better than I look," he said, slurring the words.

Brent didn't quite believe him, but he decided to use Jack's desire to cling to consciousness to his own benefit.

"Okay, then, you hold this shirt against the wound while I look for a first aid kit," Brent said.

He watched while Jack pressed hard against the wound on his leg. He frowned and concentrated on his effort. Satisfied that Jack could manage the task, Brent set to digging through the boxes.

"There's so much crap in here, maybe we'll get lucky," he muttered under his breath. The first box was stuffed with outdated electronics – answering machines, beepers and pagers, a Walkman or two. "It's like a museum in here. Every obsolete electronic device known to man."

He moved on to the next box, which held a record player. Tossing it aside, he tore into the third, glancing over at Jack. He was hunched over his leg, his elbows bent as he strained.

"How's the leg doing?" Brent asked.

"Just fine," Jack mumbled.

The next couple of boxes were packed with more useless items. Brent kicked at the boxes in frustration. He ran a hand through his hair and crossed toward the door.

"I think I saw a shed in the next yard over," Brent said. "I'll be back in less than five minutes."

Jack mumbled something in agreement and watched as Brent grabbed his rifle and slipped quietly out the door.

Jack looked down at the gaping hole in his thigh. He was losing too much blood. How had he gotten himself into this mess? He should be home by now. Home with Annie.

A few minutes later, Brent bustled in the door again. He knelt at Jack's side and prepared his supplies – a small bottle of vodka and some kind of bags stuffed full of assorted odds and ends. When he began to pull out sewing supplies, he looked up at Jack. Then he quickly looked away.

"This is the best I could find," Brent offered. "It's not going to be fun. But at least you're not going to die."

When Brent began to thread a sewing needle, Jack's stomach twisted in dread. He looked away. He wished he had lost consciousness already.

JACK OPENED his eyes and blinked confusedly. The light filtering through the tiny window was much dimmer than before.

Had he fallen asleep?

He looked down at his leg. It was throbbing with pain, but a white shirt was wrapped around the wound. It had stopped bleeding.

"Did you finally wake up?"

Jack twisted around to see Brent, who was leaned against the wall in the corner. Brent looked exhausted, with dark circles under his eyes and his hair all disheveled.

"How long was I out?" Jack asked groggily.

"Couple of hours," Brent said. "It's getting dark. Must be around 6:00 or 7:00 p.m."

Jack looked down at the jacket draped around his shoulders.

"I found some clothes in the shed next door," Brent said. "Keeping the patient warm is important when treating shock. At least, I think that's what I heard one time."

"Did you sew me up?"

Brent nodded. "And I did a damned fine job of it, too. I think when this is all over, I have a bright future in medicine waiting for me."

Jack shifted in his seat, grimacing from the pain. He

seemed to have injuries all over now. "Thanks for that, Brent. I appreciate you watching my back like that."

Brent shrugged. "You've only done it for me a half-dozen times."

"Well, you've come a long way from where you were at in LA," Jack said. He glanced at the window. "Has anyone passed through the alley?"

"Not a soul. We're lucky no one heard us back there when the guard stabbed you."

Jack shook his head. "I don't think he was a guard."

"Why not?"

"Didn't you see the way he was cowering there, hiding out of sight? Guards around here aren't like that."

Brent nodded, thinking. "You've got a point. And I guess he would have had a rifle if he'd been a guard, too."

"Exactly. He was probably hiding out there for who knows how long. He was hungry and scared. He probably thought *we* were guards."

Brent chuckled. "I guess our impersonations of the guards were a little *too* good."

Jack looked down at the shirt tied around his leg. "I guess so."

He looked out the window at the fading light of the afternoon and sighed. "The day's almost over and we still haven't found Naomi," he said, not bothering to hide the defeat in his voice.

He couldn't help feeling a little defeated, or at least frustrated. This rescue mission was supposed to have been over by now. He had underestimated the enormity of the gang's operation – both the size of their territory and the number of guards and weapons they had on their side. Once again, he was amazed at how much Oscar's gang had accomplished in just a few days. And the gang had even continued without its leader! Apparently, when one leader had been killed, another sprung up in its place, ready to rule.

"They've got way more prisoners than I ever dreamed," Brent said. "They killed a ton of people to take over this town, then enslaved the rest."

"There's just no end to man's depravity," Jack muttered.

"What did you say?" Brent asked.

Jack looked up. "I was just thinking how depraved and sick you'd have to be to do all this, to organize all this. You're right – it's slavery what they're doing. And they found so many people to go along with it, to back them up."

Brent nodded. "You should have seen the way they treated us in those dorms. They shot anyone who tried to escape. Beat us if we didn't work fast enough. We were expendable. Barely human. If they killed us, there were plenty more willing to do the work – people who'd do anything to stay alive." He looked at the bruises on Jack's face and shoulder. "Looks like you took some hits in C Block before you got out of there."

"You could say that," Jack agreed.

"How'd you get out of there, anyway? That must've been hell. Isn't C Block like their high-security prison?

"It was mostly luck. Some strategy, too, but luck had a lot to do with it."

"What was your strategy?"

"Just take one of them down at a time. And start running away as soon as they're down."

Brent laughed. "You make it sound so easy."

"It's never easy taking a man's life," Jack said. "But if it comes down to a choice between me or them, it's not as hard as you might think."

"And in a way, the rage helps, too," Brent added. "You

know, the anger that makes it possible to do things you normally wouldn't."

"In this kind of situation, I guess it's helpful," Jack agreed.

"I was so mad when that guy stabbed you, I didn't even stop to think. I just hit him," Brent said.

Jack nodded. The truth was, he was tired of fighting. He was tired of bloodshed. But as long as there were tyrants threatening his freedom and that of the people close to him, he knew he'd have to fight.

Going back out there, facing the gang and their guards, wouldn't be easy. Each confrontation meant putting his life, and now Brent's, on the line. But Jack knew they had to do it.

"So that's what we'll have to do when we go back out there, right?" Brent asked. "Just take them down one at a time?"

"Not exactly. This time will be a little different."

"How so?" Brent asked as he leaned forward.

"First, did you get a good look at the lay of the land out there when you were looking through the sheds?"

Brent smiled. "I had a feeling you'd ask me that. Yes, I did. I figured it'd be important, especially since it was starting to get dark."

"Good," Jack said. "Now, I need you to tell me everything you know."

25

Paul woke with a start. He sat bolt upright in his makeshift bed, looking around nervously.

For a second, he had forgotten where he was. He had forgotten everything. Then, with a sudden agonizing blow, he remembered it all.

It was the middle of the night, and he was still in the cornfield. He was still all alone. But his dream stayed with him, haunting him.

He had dreamed that Jack was dead.

It had been so vivid, so real, that for a second, Paul thought he was actually there, watching his brother be shot.

In his dream, Jack had gone into a tall building. He was armed, and had charged in like a movie hero. But his enemies had been waiting for him, and they pumped him full of lead until his body lay lifeless on the floor.

But it was just a dream, Paul told himself.

He wiped the sweat from his forehead and kicked the blanket off his legs. Even though the temperature had dropped while he slept, he was wet with perspiration and burning hot.

Had it been a dream, or a premonition?

Paul lay back down on the hard ground with only a blanket he had found in the empty house for padding. It had just been a bad dream. Paul hadn't spoken to his brother for years. There was no way that Paul could have a sixth sense about his estranged brother's death.

But wouldn't that just be Paul's luck – to walk halfway across Texas only to find Jack gone, or dead? Paul had already lost so much. He needed his brother to still be alive.

His mind wandered to the two brothers' falling out. They had disagreed about what to do with their mother in her final years. Jack had always denied it, but he was their mother's favorite. Everything that Jack wanted, Mom had agreed to. Jack wanted her to have in-home care when she grew too old and weak to care for herself. No one had listened to Paul's reasoning for wanting to put her in a home, where it would be safer and she'd have access to specialized care.

Paul felt his face become hot just thinking about the troubled memories. What had started as a simple disagreement had turned into an immense rift between the brothers. And in the end, Paul had lost Jack.

It seemed so silly now – losing a family member over a disagreement. Paul thought of how he and his wife had fought so much in the past two years. Was it all Paul's fault somehow? Was he just impossible to get along with?

He stood up, wanting to stretch his legs. Sleep was eluding him. He strode along the outer row of corn, which had yet to be harvested. In the darkness, he could only make out vague shapes of the tall stalks.

At the end of the row of corn, he looked out on the empty field before him. The tall grass waved in the slight breeze. Overhead, the clouds slowly parted. The silvery moonlight gradually cut through the clouds, casting the field in an eerie light and making the darkened forms in the field come into focus.

Paul jumped.

Far away, a woman stood in the field. His pulse racing, Paul stared at her silhouette.

It was Marie. It was his wife.

His throat seized up, shutting off his air supply. He looked away, stricken with terror. Anguished, he turned back to the field once more.

Nothing was there.

Paul kicked at the ground in frustration. He didn't believe in ghosts. But he was starting to believe his mind was slipping.

He hurried back to his blankets and pulled them over his head. He closed his eyes, wanting to fall asleep quickly. But even with his eyes closed, he saw his family. Their arms were reaching out toward him, begging him to help them.

He turned over in bed, trying to shut their images out. Why was his brain torturing him like this?

Gradually, he started to doze off once more. But again, he jerked awake violently, disturbed by the image of his dead brother.

What if Jack really was dead?

What if Paul made it all the way to the ranch house, only to find it deserted?

As worrisome as that thought was, Paul had yet more pressing dilemmas. He was starting to doubt his own sanity. And why not? After all, he had a mental breakdown for a day or two. After finding his family crushed dead under the rubble of their house, he had wandered in the woods aimlessly. He hadn't known where he was. He had completely lost touch with reality.

Paul had never had problems with mental illness before.

Neither had anyone in his family. So why was this happening to him now?

He lay still underneath the blanket, praying feverishly that he wouldn't lose his mind.

26

It was an hour after nightfall when Jack and Brent left the shed.

Moving under cover of night, they headed south through the alley. During Brent's search for medical supplies and clothing, he had spotted a large work crew of female prisoners two blocks away. Their housing was probably nearby, which meant they had a good chance of finding Naomi. According to Brent, the prisoners were corralled to their dorms just after dark, where they were fed. The gang ran things on a tight schedule. Now that they were without electricity, daylight was never wasted. The prisoners were brought out to work as soon as the sun rose, which meant they were sent to bed early.

If the female prisons were run like Brent's prison had been, Naomi's group would be just finishing dinner around then.

Brent directed Jack to take a turn toward the right at the end of the second block. He had spotted a three-story office building earlier. With any luck, the building would be empty, and Jack and Brent could make their way to the roof.

There, they would have a prime view of the hotel across the street.

At the end of the block, they stopped and looked at the hotel. Sure enough, both male and female guards patrolled the area. Some of them wore headlamps, and others stood in the darkness.

Judging from the presence of several female guards, the hotel was serving as a women's prison.

Keeping to the shadows, they ran up the steps of the office building. The glass doors had been broken, but no one had bothered to board them up. Hopefully that meant that the gang was not using the building.

The two men crunched the glass underfoot as they entered the building. The interior had been graffitied and destroyed. Jack and Brent walked past broken furniture and ransacked boxes on their way to the stairwell.

They climbed the stairs quickly. Jack wanted to get this over with as fast as possible. But he had to be careful, too. He was fully aware of the danger of the situation. Brent's quiet, somber attitude conveyed his understanding of just how dangerous this mission was.

The stairs opened to the third floor. Jack was disappointed there was no roof access, but maybe it was better this way. They could take cover behind the walls and aim their rifles out the windows of the third floor.

They would pick the guards off sniper style.

They walked to the southernmost office, which was an open floor plan dotted with vandalized workstations. Jack positioned himself behind a small window that had been left open. Brent chose to set up a few yards away, aiming the barrel of his rifle out a busted-out window.

"You remember what to do, right?" Jack asked, breaking the silence of the dark office.

Brent nodded. "Stay calm, keep covered, and get out of here as soon as the guards are down."

"Right. And if I get hit, don't waste any time. Just clear out of here no matter what. Find a place to hide until things calm down, then head north to the interstate."

"I remember," Brent said evenly.

"Good," Jack said, turning his eyes toward the guards below. "Are you ready?"

Brent took a deep breath. "Ready."

Jack aimed at a man holding a flashlight who paced back and forth along the sidewalk across the street. Brent trained his rifle on a large guy wearing a headlamp nearby.

Jack moved his finger from the trigger guard to the trigger.

He steadied himself, focusing all his concentration on that man's chest down there. Not only his concentration, but his outrage and fury, too. These people couldn't be allowed to get away with all they were doing. This was Jack's chance to set things straight. Not just for Naomi, but for all the people trapped in this town.

He pulled on the trigger and felt the recoil slamming the rifle against his shoulder.

Down below, the man fell to the ground.

Brent began firing. As Jack anticipated, his aim was terrible.

The guards scattered, running for cover and reaching for their weapons.

Jack chose another guard – the fastest of the bunch, who had already begun firing toward the third-story office building. Jack missed, going too high on the first few rounds. Finally, though, he hit his target, and the man fell to his knees, then collapsed on the ground.

Brent's target had run behind a car and begun firing at

Brent. The man's aim was good, and Jack turned his rifle toward this guard. When the man next raised himself to take aim after reloading, Jack hit him in the head.

Jack turned toward the man in the left end of the parking lot who was shooting toward Jack. But while he was focused on this target, Jack saw movement in his peripheral vision.

A tall, chubby guard circled around the parking lot and began to cross the street toward the office building. His intentions were clear – he was planning to attack Brent and Jack in their sniper's nest.

Jack swiveled his rifle toward the man and tried to aim, but he was too late. He had already disappeared out of sight. In moments, he would be entering the building. And maybe he would bring backup.

Brent continued firing at the man in the parking lot, getting closer to his target. To Jack's surprise, one of Brent's rounds hit the guard. The man stumbled and fell backward, his rifle crashing against the asphalt.

Jack knew they were running out of time. They would have to leave their posts and face the attack that he knew was coming from behind.

But first, he turned his sights on a man who had snuck across the street, unnoticed at first. The man was sending bullets through the brick walls and getting dangerously close to Jack's position.

Jack opened fire on the man, breaking the glass of the vehicle the man crouched behind. For a moment, there was no return fire.

Was he down? Reloading?

A barrage of bullets pummeled from the rifle down below once more. Jack struggled to keep up with the guy. Flying debris from the bullets blasting through the bricks got in Jack's eyes. He blinked, keeping his focus on the man below.

The guy raised up just a little too much, exposing his upper chest through the vehicle window for a split second before he ducked down. Jack was too quick, though. He put a bullet in the guy's chest.

Jack glanced over at Brent, who was reloading with shaking hands.

"We've got to get out of here!" Jack shouted over the roar of bullets pounding into the brick wall. "They're on their way up now."

Brent crawled away from the window and pushed himself to his feet. He looked over at Jack.

Jack gave one last glance toward the hotel below. What he saw made him do a double take. Brent turned to get one last look as well.

A stream of female prisoners had began rushing out the front entrance of the hotel. Wielding weapons of every description – knives, shovels, folding chairs – they descended upon the guards.

As their enslavers continued shooting toward the office building, the prisoners crept up silently, fanning out through the street and parking lot.

Then, they attacked.

Two women beat a male guard with shovels. Nearby a young woman plunged a kitchen knife in the back of another guard. Across the parking lot, a female prisoner let out a war cry as she lunged at a guard with a rifle she had picked up off a downed guard. She hit the guard over the head with the rifle, then ran off to the south, disappearing from the scene.

Jack and Brent watched as more women ran screaming

from the hotel, adding to the chaos of the scene below as they charged at the people who had tortured them.

A rebellion was beginning.

Footsteps in the stairwell broke their trance. Jack motioned for Brent to follow him toward the door.

The two men hid behind the open door to the south office, out of sight. They listened as the man exited the stairwell and moved slowly through the hallway. Within seconds, the overweight guard stepped in the office, panting for his breath. His rifle was raised. He was clearly expecting to take care of the snipers easily.

From behind the door, Jack kicked the door out and made contact with the guard, who dropped his rifle.

The guard began to crawl on his knees, lunging at his gun. But Jack kicked the man square in his belly.

The guard slumped on the floor, groaning in pain. Brent appeared at Jack's side. Brent stared at the guard for a moment. Then in one sudden, frenetic movement, he hit the man's head with his rifle.

Jack grabbed the man's rifle and hurried over to the hallway to look for any more guards. He waited and listened for a moment, then went to the stairwell. It was empty.

He returned to the office. Something had snapped in Brent. He had lost control of himself and he was beating the man over and over with the gun.

Jack grabbed his arm before he could lower the rifle on the man's body again. Brent looked up at Jack.

"Let it go," Jack said.

Brent looked down at the man and blinked, rousing himself from his trance. The guard was unconscious.

He followed Jack to the window, where they watched the unfolding scene of the rebellion.

Women continue to attack the guards, though there

were very few guards standing anymore. A few new guards came running up, having heard the outbreak. But they were ambushed by the women, who now were armed with guns. They shot down several guards. Another group of guards, late to arrive on the scene, saw what was happening, and fled in the other direction. Three armed women took off after them, chasing them down the street.

Jack kept his eyes on the front doors, hoping to see Naomi. But woman after woman escaped, until only a few stragglers emerged from the building now and then. But Naomi never appeared.

The female inmates ran off in every direction, crazed by the excitement of the rebellion and their newfound freedom. Most of them scattered in random directions, seemingly unsure where to go.

But Jack noticed a group of about five women run from the hotel and head south in a determined way. They ran uphill, evidently focused on a predetermined location. They knew where they were going, unlike all the others.

The group disappeared out of sight, scrambling up the street on a mission.

Brent sighed. "I guess Naomi isn't in this hotel. How many women's prisons could they possibly have?"

But Jack didn't answer. He was focused on the sudden noise of engines starting. Several blocks to the south, two or three vehicles cut through the noise of the violence breaking out down below.

"Let's go," Jack said, turning and running toward the stairs. "They're going after the cars."

27

Naomi was on cleanup duty again.

In the dark, dingy kitchen of the motel where she was kept prisoner, she worked by candlelight to wash stacks of dishes. Joanne poured water sparingly from one-gallon bottles in short spurts as needed, just enough for Naomi to scrub the food from the plates.

If Joanne was a little too liberal with the water, the guards barked at them.

"Conserve water!" the guard known as Morticia screamed. "Don't you idiots know we have to conserve water! Do you think we can just turn on the tap when we need more?"

"Sorry," Joanne said nervously. When the guard turned her back, Joanne rolled her eyes at Naomi.

Naomi gave a weak smile at her friend. Joanne was the only person who made this nightmare bearable. If the older woman hadn't been so kind to her, Naomi would already have been dead. More and more, Naomi was depending on Joanne's support.

Naomi glanced over at Brooke, who worked cleaning the

knives nearby. Brooke gave Naomi a smug, condescending smile. She was gratified whenever the other inmates got in trouble. Brooke was a fellow prisoner, but she had kissed up to the guards enough to get special privileges, like less work and bigger portions of food. She was the only one allowed to use and clean the kitchen knives. Fearing attack, the guards didn't trust anyone else with them.

Naomi looked back at the plate she was scrubbing, then nodded for Joanne to pour the water while she held it to be rinsed clean. Dinner was over, but she was still hungry. The food rations were much too small for the amount of work these people expected.

Naomi grabbed another dish, this one encrusted with dried food bits. She felt her stomach turn, both from revulsion and hunger pains.

Across the room, four other prisoners worked at the big, industrial sink, scrubbing pots and pans. A couple of women nearby worked to clean the gas stove, and another pair of women washed dishes at a third sink in the corner. Two or three other prisoners put the food away and swept the floor. Four female guards patrolled the women as they worked.

If they were anything, the guards were organized. They demanded order and tidiness from the prisoners at all times. They ran a tight ship, and their intolerance for any deviation from orders seemed to be a tool they wielded. The guards expected total obedience, and anything less was viewed as insubordination and would be punished.

A loud noise from outside startled the women, making Naomi jump and nearly drop the plate. A wave of relief washed over her when she caught the dish in time. After all, breaking something would result in a beating.

But what was that noise? Was it a gunshot?

Several more loud bangs made their way through the dark kitchen, then the noise grew louder.

Naomi and Joanne looked at each other, then around the kitchen at the dozen or so other female inmates. They stared at each other silently as if to ask the same question.

What was going on out there?

"Back to work!" Morticia hissed, glaring at them. "Do you think I wanna stand around here all night while you silly girls make eyes at each other?"

The women returned to their labor, keeping their eyes down. But outside, the noise increased in volume all at once.

It was definitely the sound of guns. Rifles, probably.

And every moment, there seemed to be more guns firing. Naomi felt her heart pick up its pace as she listened. It sounded like a war zone outside.

It was hard to discern where the noise was coming from because of its echo through the hills. But the roar of the gunfire was so deafening that it couldn't have been very far away.

Naomi stood frozen, listening. She met Joanne's eyes, and they both stared at each other in disbelief.

"Get back to work, now!" Morticia yelled, breaking herself out of her own trance as she listened. Naomi could hear the rising frantic edge in the guard's voice.

Outside, the battle raged on.

She felt a small, stubborn bit of hope deep within herself. Something big was happening out there.

But a sudden blow against her ribs knocked all the optimism out of her. The guard had suddenly elbowed her in the back. Naomi felt the wind forced out of her chest.

"Don't let me catch you slacking off again," Morticia screamed at Naomi inches from her ear.

Naomi hurried to resume washing the dishes, disgusted

by her own cowardice. If she had been brave, she would be able to stand up to that guard. She remembered how she had stoically faced the guard's abuse before. But now, after carrying the scars and bruises, she was afraid. Now, when push came to shove, she would do anything to avoid provoking their violence.

"Are you okay?" Joanne muttered under her breath when the guard had turned away.

Naomi nodded her head as the pain washed over her. The sooner they finished, the sooner they could take refuge in their own rooms.

She darted her eyes over at Brooke, who was drying a chef's knife with a dish towel. Brooke seemed on edge like the rest of them, and she snuck furtive glances at the guards supervising the women's work.

Suddenly, a wailing noise from outside filled the air.

Again, the women in the kitchen stopped their work and looked at each other. Naomi caught a glimpse of fear on Morticia's face.

It took Naomi a moment to realize what the this new wailing sound was. It was the sound of women screaming at the top of their lungs.

The prisoners were escaping.

The sound came from the big hotel several blocks away. Naomi had seen the hotel earlier that day, from a distance. It was another female prison.

Could it really be happening?

The voices rose in intensity, some of them growing louder as the women ran in every direction through the neighborhood.

Yes, it was true. The women were rebelling.

Naomi looked down at the plate she was holding. Her hands were shaking so much that she nearly dropped it.

Placing it in the sink, she snuck a glance at the scene nearby to her left.

In an erratic frenzy, Morticia lunged at Brooke, who was carefully drying a sharp knife.

"Give those to me!" Morticia screamed.

The guard snatched up the case of knives from the table. She grabbed the chef's knife from Brooke's hands. Brooke watched in surprise and fear. Morticia worked furiously to pack the blades away in the folding wooden case.

Meanwhile, Naomi heard bits of murmured communication among the women in the room as they stared, wide-eyed, at each other.

"We have to do something," Joanne said under her breath to Naomi.

"Keep quiet!" another guard roared, stepping toward the middle of the room. "I don't want to hear another peep out of any of you!"

"Get them to their rooms!" a third guard called angrily from the back of the kitchen.

Two of the guards reached for the nearest prisoners and began snapping handcuffs around their wrists. One woman was cuffed to the stove while the guard moved on to the next prisoner.

Nearby, Morticia slammed the case shut and stashed it in a high cabinet. She moved to fit the padlock around the chain and secure the cabinet. She strained to reach overhead as she positioned the chain.

Just then, a prisoner lunged at the guard, bringing a heavy skillet down against Morticia's head.

And that was when Naomi lost track of what was happening.

Confusion was breaking out all around her. Morticia stumbled forward, grabbing hold of the counter's edge to keep her balance. Her attacker reached toward the cabinet where the knives were stashed. Several women screamed in the room as a guard drew her handgun.

"Get down!" Joanne screamed.

Joanne ducked down by the sink, pulling Naomi to the floor with her.

An enormous *bang* filled the room. Naomi felt her heart lurch as she and Joanne crouched as low they could.

Just a few feet away, the woman who had attacked Morticia gasped. A moment later, she fell to the floor. Her body hit the tiles with a thud. The dead woman's eyes stared lifelessly in Naomi's direction.

Naomi felt paralyzed as she looked around the room in confusion. Some of the prisoners were struggling with the guards, trying to wrench their guns out of their hands. One prisoner grabbed a guard's rifle just before the guard could shoot her with it. The prisoner ripped it out of her hands and bashed the guard's head.

A moment later, that prisoner was shot dead by a third guard. Meanwhile, another guard was handcuffing the prisoners, one by one. The guard was headed toward the four women at the big sink nearby.

Naomi looked up at Morticia. She was hanging on to consciousness by a thin thread, and she fell to her knees. She wavered unsteadily, then slumped down to the floor.

Joanne looked at Naomi.

"Now's our chance," Joanne whispered. "We have to get out of here before they send more guards in."

She began to crawl along the floor toward Morticia. Looking around her to make sure no guards were watching, she silently reached for her rifle. Joanne clumsily held the firearm and rose to her feet, still crouching and unsure what to do with the gun at first. But she quickly found her bearings, and pointed the gun toward the guard nearby.

Across the room, the fourth guard scanned the room. Any moment now, she would notice Joanne's movements.

"Wait!" Naomi whispered to Joanne.

But Joanne had already lifted the rifle and was aiming at the nearest guard.

Joanne pulled the trigger long and hard, showering the guard with bullets. That guard fell to the floor.

The prisoners nearby screamed and ducked.

The fourth guard pivoted toward Joanne.

"No!" Naomi screamed.

Before Joanne could turn toward the final guard, another round of bullets tore through the room.

Joanne's body jumped and twitched. The rifle clattered to the floor.

Naomi stared at her in disbelief. She didn't notice as the final guard stomped across the room and snatched up the rifle.

She only stared at her friend. Joanne was still alive, but only barely. She stared upward. Naomi moved to the older woman's side.

"Please hold on," Naomi said. "Don't leave me!"

Joanne's lips were moving. Naomi brought her ear close to her mouth so she could hear her faint whisper.

"You have to run," Joanne whispered. "Get free."

Naomi shook her head. Her mind raced. She had to do something.

"No, Joanne. Don't talk like that, okay? You're going to make it."

She began to apply pressure to one of the holes in Joanne's body. The blood spurted out over her hands. She moved frantically, unsure of what to do to save her friend.

Finally, she looked at Joanne's face. Her eyes were unblinking and glassy.

She was gone.

Naomi felt herself go numb. The sights and sounds of the chaos both inside and outside of that kitchen fell away. There was commotion erupting all around her, but she paid it no attention.

She only stared at Joanne's face, the face of the woman who had meant so much to her, who had saved her life.

Naomi had found a stand-in for her own mother in Joanne, and Naomi had been a reminder to Joanne of the daughter she had lost. This woman's kindness had been the only thing that kept Naomi fighting to stay alive, the only reason she had to stay alive.

Now all that was lost.

She became aware of a voice shouting at her. There was someone standing nearby, demanding Naomi do something. Naomi could hear the brutality in the voice, the willingness to end Naomi's life without a second thought.

But Naomi felt no concern. Why should she?

She felt herself leave her own body and begin to watch the scene from above. She saw herself huddled over Joanne's lifeless form, and the guard screaming at her.

She hoped it would all be over soon.

28

Charlotte watched as Annie tore out of the tiny little town.

"Annie, are you okay?" Charlotte asked nervously.

Annie didn't answer. She gripped the steering wheel tightly and leaned forward in her seat.

She felt her chest tighten and constrict, forcing her to take shallow breaths.

Why was Loretta empty? What if there had been some kind of biological weapon used on the area? Maybe everyone had died in their houses!

Or maybe that was unrealistic. Maybe something even worse had happened. What if there was someone already at the old Hawthorne house?

Annie recalled the squatters who had moved in to her own house in Austin, destroying her things and living there as if they owned the place.

Perhaps people had already moved into the ranch house. It had happened at the house with the horse – a drug addict had murdered the inhabitants and moved in!

If Annie and Charlotte drove up to the ranch house, they were liable to get ambushed.

Then the darkest thought of all crossed Annie's mind.

Suppose Jack had found a way to the ranch house and arrived earlier, only to be murdered in his sleep by thieves scavenging for anything of value?

Annie's throat went dry and her jaw ached with tension. Could it really be possible? Could Jack already be dead?

"Annie!" Charlotte said, breaking her thoughts momentarily. "I'm worried about you! Talk to me, please."

"I'm okay," Annie said. "Just a little nervous about the house. I've got a bad feeling about it."

Charlotte watched as Annie swerved around an abandoned car in the middle of the road.

"Well, could you slow down?" Charlotte asked, bracing herself in her seat. "You're not a NASCAR driver."

"Sorry," Annie said as she eased up on the gas pedal a bit. "I just want to get there already."

"I do too, but I want to get there in one piece." Charlotte glanced at Annie's face, which was rapidly turning bright red. "What's going on in that head of yours?"

"I'm worried about someone being in the house," Annie blurted out. "Someone who doesn't belong where."

Charlotte nodded. "I can understand that, especially after your run-in with that drug addict back there. Do you want to discuss strategy?"

Annie shook her head. "No strategy."

"Well, I think you can at least take a few deep breaths. You look like you're about to hyperventilate."

Annie tried to draw a slow breath to fill her lungs, but it ended up being more of a gasp. She clenched the steering wheel harder. The scenery was flying past, all blending together in one indistinguishable blur. The visual imagery speeding by reminded her of the confusion of the past few days.

Where would she and Charlotte go if the Hawthorne house was filled with squatters? She had already lost her Austin house – not that she wanted to return to the city now, with its gun battles, fires, and looting. Not to mention all the people who would try to steal the Porsche.

But still, where was home now? Even if the ranch house were empty, even if it was relatively safe, how would they survive? Annie didn't know how to grow all her own food. Winter was around the corner, which meant the growing season would be coming to an end soon. What would they eat and drink?

There were so many unanswered questions. So many ways it all could go wrong. She and Charlotte would be two women alone in an isolated property. They would be so easy to rob, attack, or kill.

She had lost control of her life in ways she had never imagined. She didn't know if her husband was alive or dead. She didn't know about her family. Maybe she would never see any of them again. Even with the Porsche, how would she find Jack? And how could she ever drive all the way out to Tennessee or Virginia to find her family? Everything was so dangerous now. She would never make it out east. It had been so hard just covering the two hundred miles between Austin and Loretta. She would be killed before she could get halfway across Texas.

And it wasn't just her life she had lost control of – she had lost sight of the entire world. She didn't know what to think anymore. There was nothing left to trust in. It was almost like she could no longer trust reality itself.

She was feeling dizzy. She was losing sense of which way

was up. She just knew that it was becoming more and more difficult to breathe, and everything was coming at her faster.

"Annie! You're going too fast again!" Charlotte shouted, alarmed at Annie's speed.

But Annie didn't hear her.

She just kept driving. She had to get there. She had to find out for herself if the house was empty.

"Annie, stop!" Charlotte pleaded. "Let me drive. You're freaking me out."

"I have to see the house," Annie muttered. "We're almost there. Just one more mile."

Charlotte groaned and covered her eyes with her hands, not wanting to see the reckless way Annie was driving.

Annie weighed her options. When they got there, should she pull into the long driveway, or park on the highway and walk in? If she drove close to the house, they might be trapped if there were squatters inside. And a confrontation would likely be deadly.

If she parked on the highway, she might have to try to make her way to the house stealthily, without being seen. But then she ran the risk of having the Porsche stolen while she was away from it.

"Look out!" Charlotte screamed.

An abandoned SUV in the middle of the road came into view as they scaled the final hill.

Without thinking, Annie slammed on the brakes and pulled the steering wheel hard to the left. The Porsche swerved and the tires squealed, and Annie tried hard to maintain control.

Objects flew past in her peripheral vision as Charlotte screamed beside her.

29

Naomi was startled by someone's hands grabbing her shoulders and shaking her.

She blinked, coming out of her dissociative state. She looked at the prisoner's face in front of her, just inches from her own. The woman's mouth was open. She was yelling something at Naomi.

Finally, the sound of her voice reached Naomi's ears. It was still fuzzy, as if moving through a dream, but Naomi could hear her at last.

"Go! Run, Naomi! Run!"

The prisoner let go of Naomi's shoulders and ran out the kitchen door. For a moment, Naomi looked around. The guard who had been screaming at Naomi before was lying dead at her feet. Someone had shot her.

A few other bodies lay dead in the kitchen. Prisoners and guards. Naomi did a quick count of the guards. Four of them lay on the floor. Most of the prisoners had already escaped.

Naomi was all alone in the room.

Suddenly, she was filled with an urgent fear. At any

moment, more guards could enter the room and drag Naomi off someplace, handcuffed and unable to fight. If Naomi didn't move now, she would be trapped again.

She pushed open the swinging kitchen doors and looked in the hallway.

Several female prisoners were running out of rooms and down the stairs. Everyone was headed to the front door. Upstairs, guns were being fired. There were still guards in the motel. Naomi ran into the hallway, following the women running toward the front door.

As she got closer to the exit, she could hear the sound of several rifles being fired outside the building. She saw women being pelted with bullets as they ran outside the motel.

What should she do?

She turned and looked back down the hall. Behind her, a guard was just kicking open a door and emerging. The woman was enraged and screaming at the prisoners. She raised her rifle.

Naomi felt a wave of panic surge through her. She had two choices, and they both involved running toward an armed, and furious, guard.

30

Jack and Brent moved down the stairs of the office building quietly. They didn't want to alert anyone who might be hiding in wait of their presence.

They emerged from the building cautiously. Jack wanted to move faster, but he fought the urge within himself to break into a run across the street. There was still violence breaking out around the hotel. They would have to move carefully through the area.

Across the street, a few prisoners charged across the parking lot toward a female guard. The guard opened fire on two of them, killing the women. But the remaining two women hit the guard with shovels. A third prisoner shot the guard.

Another small group of prisoners streamed out of the hotel and headed toward the south, in the direction of the vehicles.

Jack kept his weapons ready as he made his way down the sidewalk. He glanced over at the bodies surrounding the hotel. Many prisoners had been shot, but the body count of the guards was larger.

They skirted around the hotel until they reached the road that ran adjacent to the hotel. Turning to the right, Jack headed south.

"We've got to get one of the cars before it's too late," he said over his shoulder to Brent as the two men picked up speed on the quieter street.

"What about Naomi?" Brent asked. "We're just going to leave her behind?"

"Of course not," Jack said. "We're going to look for her. But if we don't get a vehicle now, they'll be all gone."

The two men broke into a sprint once they were past the hotel area. Jack was still on alert. The danger of being attacked by a stray guard was still high, and he was on the lookout for any anomalies in the shadowy street.

Behind them, more and more escaped prisoners headed south. Headlights came over the hill. They dodged a vehicle speeding down the road. It was a vintage pickup truck. Jack's chest tightened with worry. Hopefully, there would still be some vehicles left by the time they got there.

Once they cleared the hill, they saw a small covered parking garage where the vehicles had been kept. Two more vehicles were being driven off the lot.

Jack pushed himself to run faster, leaving Brent struggling to keep up. He passed a trio of escaped prisoners who were also headed to the cars.

Jack could only hope that the keys would be in the vehicles.

Once they got to the garage, Jack was relieved to see three vehicles parked there. He had only moments to find a vehicle and drive off before more prisoners arrived.

The Pathfinder was gone, but a couple of old 1970s sedans and a late 1980s Chevy Bronco remained. Jack sprinted across the parking lot toward the Bronco.

The vehicle was unlocked, but the keys were nowhere to be found. Gritting his teeth and clenching his jaw, he searched through the glove box, through the back seats, under the floor mats, and behind the visors.

He spun around, looking through the space. He could hear the voices of the escaped prisoners approaching.

Jack couldn't lose this chance to get a running vehicle.

As he sprinted toward the first old car, a run-down Pinto, a small lockbox mounted on the wall nearby in the corner caught his eye. Throwing open the hinged door to the box, he felt his heart burst with relief.

Three sets of keys hung from hooks.

He grabbed the Bronco keys and returned to the Chevy just as the prisoners entered the garage.

Jack turned the keys and the Bronco purred.

He backed the vehicle out of the spot and drove past the prisoners who were descending upon the remaining two cars. Brent ran inside the garage. Jack came to a quick stop, just long enough for Brent to climb in.

Jack turned east down a side street as Brent slammed the door shut and glanced at him.

"Nice work, Jack," Brent said. "It's even better than the Pathfinder."

"Save it for later," Jack said. "For now, be on the lookout for any guards. Be prepared to return fire."

Brent swallowed nervously, then readied his rifle, pointing the barrel skyward out the window. Keeping low, he positioned himself to have a good view of the area outside.

"If you see any groups of women, let me know that too," Jack instructed. "We've got to find Naomi."

Jack turned left and drove north on the next large street.

"There's a big group of people a couple blocks down on

the right," Brent said quickly. "Can't tell if they're friends or foes yet."

Brent's uncertainty was answered quickly as two guards began shooting at the Bronco.

Jack ducked and swerved the vehicle to the left. He aimed his Glock out the window and began shooting in their direction. He knew he didn't have a good vantage point to have any kind of accuracy, but at least it would hold them back a little.

In the passenger seat, Brent opened fire on the group of male guards. As they got closer, the guards stopped shooting as they tried to avoid Brent's return fire. Jack made a quick right on the next street, turning away from the men. The guards made a half-hearted attempt to shoot after the Bronco as it cleared the intersection, but Jack and Brent quickly were out of range.

Brent exhaled roughly. With shaking hands, he reloaded the rifle, then returned to his vigil as they drove through the neighborhood.

"Turn to the left at the next block," Brent said quickly. "I see a bunch of women down there. They're all running out of some building."

Jack followed Brent's instructions and charged down the next street. Sure enough, a group of escaped prisoners were flooding out of a small motel. The women ran frantically out the front door, screaming in terror as guns were being fired from within the building.

Across the street, guards hiding out of sight opened fire on the women. Some of the women were hit, but many more kept running. A few escaped prisoners were armed, and they returned fire on the guards across the street.

The ones who managed to escape fled into the night,

disappearing behind buildings or in the shadows of the dark streets.

The scene was alarming. Jack debated what to do. He couldn't drive through the street where the guards were firing – it was too much of a risk. But what if Naomi was in that group?

"I see her!" Brent shouted. "She just ran out of the building!"

Jack saw Naomi slip out of the door and run off to the right, away from the approach of the Bronco. Across the street, the guards kept shooting.

Jack could only do one thing.

He stepped on the gas as he aimed his Glock out the window with his left hand. He began firing toward the guards as he drove. Brent followed his lead and and started to shoot toward the stand of trees where the guards were hiding.

The guards turned their attention to the Bronco headed their way. Jack kept low.

He glanced over toward the motel and watched as Naomi bolted away from the motel, disappearing behind the building.

Jack narrowly avoided being shot as they got closer. A couple of the female prisoners across the street took out a few of the guards, then ran off and escaped into the night.

"Hold on," Jack said to Brent. Jack floored the gas as they passed the cluster of guards. The Bronco was hit a couple of times.

But Jack and Brent were unharmed.

Jack took the next turn quickly and drove up the side street. They were out of range of the guards behind them, but they were far from safe. The street was chaotic, with prisoners and guards running in every direction. A few scattered guards were running away, scattering from the motel.

It seemed like the tide had finally turned. Now, the guards were running for their lives.

Jack slowed as he drove through the dark road. He saw several escaped prisoners running frantically, both men and women. But he didn't see Naomi.

As they crossed the next intersection, he found himself looking at the dead bodies littering the street. The more ground they covered without finding Naomi, the more he worried he might recognize one of those lifeless bodies.

31

Annie felt the brakes lock. She let off the pedal, and the car lurched forward. She corrected the vehicle just in time, straightening it out before it went sailing off the road.

The Porsche slid down the highway another hundred feet before Annie brought it to a complete stop.

She looked over at Charlotte.

"Are you okay?" Annie asked breathlessly.

Charlotte turned to her with widened eyes. "I think so."

Annie sat quietly, trying to calm her shakiness.

"I'm sorry," she said. "Everything just got out of control back there."

Charlotte nodded uneasily. Then she looked up and saw a large brick home perched on a hill off the highway to the left. "Is that it?"

Annie glanced up at the house. "That's it."

They had just passed the driveway. Annie put the car in reverse and backed up to where the front of the vehicle was in line with the gravel entrance. She came to a stop, staring at the house.

It looked empty, but they were a few hundred yards away and too far to get a good look. Annie glanced at the SUV that had been abandoned in the middle of the road nearby.

"Well, are we going to go in?" Charlotte asked wearily.

Annie nodded. "Yeah, but I don't like that SUV."

Charlotte scoffed. "I don't like it either, because we nearly ran off the road dodging it. But does that mean we have to sit here staring at it?"

Annie studied the vehicle, noting its polished exterior and luxury finishes. "They broke down out here when the EMP hit."

"Yeah. So?"

"Where did they go when they left the car behind?"

Charlotte swallowed, looking back at the SUV. She shifted uncomfortably in her seat, then looked up at the house.

"You think they're inside?" Charlotte asked in a whisper.

Annie glanced down at the pistol.

"I guess we're about to find out," she said.

Finally, she shifted the car into first gear and began to climb the long driveway.

She was tired of running. She was going to face whatever came her way head on. It was her husband's house, after all. No one else had any right to be there. She wasn't going to cower away from any squatters.

She would get them off the ranch, or die trying.

"You wait here," she told Charlotte. "I'm going to check the place out first."

Annie grabbed the pistol and got out of the car. She took a long look at the house, then walked up to the front door. It was locked.

With her heart pounding, she edged along the front yard toward the barn in the back. She knew her .22 was no match for a larger gun, and certainly not multiple guns. But she pushed herself on.

The barn was just as it had been left last time. She walked in to the large, open structure and headed for a small tackle box on a shelf. Rummaging through the odds and ends, she came upon the key that was kept hidden in the box. Placing it in her palm, she clenched it tightly as she returned to the house.

Fear was beginning to cloud her judgment now, and she considered getting in the car and driving off.

No, you're not going to run away this time.

She unlocked the door, and stepped into the dark, quiet house.

"Hello!" she called.

Her voice echoed through the halls.

She walked through the living room and kitchen. So far, nothing was out of place. She went upstairs, checking each bedroom.

The house was empty.

She walked toward the window in the master bedroom and looked outside where the SUV was stranded on the highway.

The driver must have walked somewhere else when they broke down. Maybe they lived nearby, and they had been able to make it home.

Finally, something had gone right.

Annie knew she should go down and get Charlotte, but she couldn't resist collapsing in the bed for just a moment.

She had finally made it.

She had finally reached freedom. She felt her body loosen its knots – all the tight spots she hadn't even realized she had been carrying the last few days.

But as the tension began to gradually fade, sadness took its place. Jack wasn't there.

Swallowing the lump forming in her throat, she pushed herself to her feet and went downstairs.

Outside the house, Charlotte looked at her expectantly.

"All clear!" Annie announced.

Charlotte looked relieved. She opened her car door and Annie helped her to her feet. As Charlotte slowly hobbled inside the house, Annie brought the luggage inside.

Charlotte looked around the living room and the stairs that led to the bedrooms on the second floor. "If you don't mind, I'd rather not tackle the stairs just yet."

"I don't mind at all," Annie said, helping her friend to lie down on the couch. "You can sleep here for now."

Annie finished bringing their things inside, then retrieved a large first aid kit from the bathroom.

"Time to change your dressings," Annie said as she sat on the floor at Charlotte's side.

As Annie worked, she answered Charlotte's questions about the house and the area. Charlotte had never spent much time in the Hill Country.

"All done," Annie said as she collected the empty bandage wrappers. "Your wounds are still pretty raw. But hopefully you'll be able to heal better now that we're in a more stable place."

Charlotte smiled. "Thanks, Annie. And thanks for bringing me out here. I may not always agree with your methodology, but I have to hand it to you. You got us out here when I never thought it was possible."

Annie smiled back at her friend. "You're welcome. Thanks for coming along for the ride."

She collapsed in the recliner nearby, curling her legs up. She glanced at Charlotte, who looked considerably less stressed. But Annie couldn't help noticing a sadness on Charlotte's face. They had fought so hard to get here, but their struggles were far from over. Charlotte knew just as well as Annie did that they weren't fully prepared to defend themselves.

Annie looked out the window at the magnolia tree in the front yard. She remembered Jack's childhood stories about playing with his brother, Paul, around that tree.

"Jack's going to get here," Charlotte said. "It might take him a while, but he'll show up. He loves you too much not to find a way."

Annie nodded. "I know," she said quietly.

Feeling tears welling up, she closed her eyes shut.

Unfortunately, love wasn't always enough. Maybe things in LA had gotten out of control. As painful as it was, Annie couldn't live her life waiting for Jack to return. No matter how much it hurt, she would have to find a way to carry on without him.

32

"Where is she?" Brent asked nervously as he rode in the Bronco through the dark streets.

Jack scanned the left side of the road as he drove. "She couldn't have gotten very far."

"Naomi!" Brent called toward a cluster of buildings off to the side. Scattered prisoners moved across the parking lot, but none of them responded to Brent's call.

Jack knew they needed to flee the area quickly. There were still guards roaming about. Though the fighting had quieted down somewhat, gunshots still echoed through the town all around them. He turned down a side street where he saw several prisoners escaping to the east.

He spotted a petite woman running across the street, driven by fear and urgency.

Could it be her?

They were still too far away to tell. Jack picked up speed as the woman crossed the street and began to run down the sidewalk.

As he drove the truck closer, the woman turned around

to glance at the approaching vehicle. The headlights shone across her face.

"It's her!" Brent said. "Naomi!"

The woman stopped, and Jack got a better look at her. Brent was right. They had finally found Naomi.

She stared at the Bronco, bewildered and blinded by the headlamps. Jack drove forward a bit, then came to a stop as Brent leaned out the window.

"It's us!" Brent exclaimed. "Get in!"

Recognition and relief washed over her face, and she lunged at the backseat door. She opened it and flung herself inside. Jack took off as she slammed the door shut.

Brent twisted around and grinned at her. Jack looked at her in the rearview mirror. She was shaken, but smiling. She sat there, catching her breath and taking it all in.

"I can't believe we found you!" Brent said. "They've got at least three women's prisons. We've been all over town searching for you."

"I can't believe it either!" Naomi said. "But how did you get out? They took you to C Block, Jack – how did you possibly escape? And how did you get this truck?"

"We're not out yet," Jack said. "We still have to make it out of this town without being shot."

Brent swiveled around to face the front and returned to his vigil at the window. "All I can say is, it was hell," Brent said in response to Naomi's questions as he readied himself.

"Are you okay, Naomi?" Jack asked, glancing at her in the mirror again.

Naomi nodded. "I think so. All things considered."

Jack continued east. As they crossed a main thoroughfare, a commotion to the south caught their attention. Another prison breakout was happening in the large hotel several blocks to the right.

Prisoners were attacking the guards. Jack saw several men running out from the hotel, whooping and hollering as they ran to freedom.

Everywhere in White Rock, the captured were breaking free. The momentum Jack had started by escaping, and what he and Brent had continued by attacking the guards, had started an uprising. Jack knew the gang's time was up. They were rapidly losing their strongholds and their power with every passing minute. Soon, justice would be restored to the city, in one way or another.

After a few blocks heading east through a residential neighborhood, Jack turned left, to the north.

"We've got about a mile till we get to the interstate," Jack said, focusing on the road. "They might have guards posted at the interstate trying to keep us from leaving the city, so everyone be ready. Get down as much as you can."

As they came within a few blocks of the interstate, Jack tensed up once more. Next to him, Brent steadied his rifle.

"Look! They're running away!" Naomi said from the backseat.

And sure enough, a band of a about fifteen guards were running underneath the interstate overpass, toward the devastated downtown area.

"They're escaping!" Brent said, frustrated. "Shouldn't we go after them? We can't let them get away. Not after everything they've done to us."

Jack watched them scurry away. Some of them were carrying a rifle or a handgun, but most of them had no weapons he could see. They were trying to make a clean break, and they looked over their shoulders as they ran.

"No," Jack said, shaking his head. "We made it this far. Let's not press our luck."

"Good point," Brent said. He remained vigilant as they turned toward the interstate and climbed the on-ramp.

"Looks like C Block is on fire," Jack said. He glanced down to see the motel that had served as his prison going up in flames.

"They're burning down a few other buildings, too," Brent said.

They all looked down toward the city, which was erupting in chaos. Several houses in the upscale residential neighborhood, where the gang's headquarters had been kept, were being consumed by fires. People ran in every direction – some escaping to freedom, and others searching for safety from the fire and the escaped prisoners. A few vehicles drove through the city and headed toward the interstate.

"So long, White Rock," Naomi said quietly from the backseat.

The Bronco accelerated quickly as they took one more look at the city. To the left, Jack saw the devastation of the downtown buildings with its blackened piles of rubble. To the right, the gang's operation was rapidly falling apart.

They drove east on the highway, covering mile after mile until they could see no trace of the city any longer.

33

"Please?" Heather asked her brother as she held a bowl of soup toward him. "Can't you eat just a little more?"

Brody shook his head slightly, refusing the food. "No thanks. I don't think I could keep it down."

Standing on the other side of the bed, Myra fidgeted nervously. "Oh, is your nausea back?"

Brody closed his eyes and nodded.

Heather and Myra exchanged a worried look. Brody had been in bed all day. He had eaten very little, complaining of nausea and dizziness.

Myra brought her hand to her son's forehead. "He's burning up again," she said to Heather.

Myra reached for the damp washcloth and placed it on Brody's forehead. She began to caress his head, but a clump of hair came loose in her hands. Alarmed, she stared at the handful of hair in her palm, then set it down on the nightstand.

"Katie?" Brody asked, his eyes still closed.

"She's still outside," Myra said. "I can go try to bring her up here if you want."

"Please."

Myra exchanged another worried glance with Heather, then she turned and walked out of the room with slumped shoulders. Heather set the bowl of soup down and looked at her brother. When Katie had seen her father that morning, she had run off outside, disappearing for hours.

Myra had finally found her earlier that day in the tallest branches of a tree at the edge of the front yard. The teenager, so disturbed by the sight of her seriously ill father, had refused to come down.

"Isn't there anything we can do, Brody?" Heather asked, leaning on the side of the bed.

Brody swallowed. "If I start to get weird again, don't let her see me like that. Okay?"

"Okay," Heather agreed.

Around noon, Brody had become delirious. He had completely lost touch with reality. He had spent an hour or two babbling incoherently, talking to his dead wife as if he could see her in the room. Myra and Heather had watched on anxiously, relieved that Katie hadn't been there to see it.

Then, when his temperature dropped a little, he had started to make sense again. But the episode had exhausted him, and he was left even weaker than before. His color had turned a more sickly shade of gray, and his eyes were bloodshot and heavily ringed with dark circles. His hands, when he could lift them, had a heavy tremor. And his voice was weak and shaky.

Heather was exhausted, but the concern for her brother pushed her on. She was frustrated with the hopelessness of the situation. If only there was something she could do for him! All she could do was sit by his side and watch him waste away, growing a little weaker by the hour.

MYRA PULLED her sweater around her as she walked to the edge of the yard. The sky had clouded over, turning the early fall day chilly. She spotted Katie perched on a long, sweeping branch of the old oak tree near the fence. The leaves had just started to change color, tingeing some of the green leaves with a golden yellow. Memories of autumns past flashed through Myra's mind as she looked at the tree.

"Your father liked to sit on the same branch when he was a kid," Myra called as she drew near. She came to a stop underneath the tree and looked up at Katie, whose face was tear-stained. "Annie, too. You look so much like your aunt up there."

"I'm not going in there!" Katie announced, crossing her arms over her chest. "I can't! I don't want to see him like that."

Myra peered upward, straining to find sight of the teenager through the tangle of branches and leaves. "Can you please come down here and talk to me?" Myra asked. "It's kind of hard to have a conversation like this."

Katie sighed, then nodded. "Okay, I'll come down."

Myra watched as her granddaughter nimbly lowered herself from branch to branch, then jumped from the lowest joint of the tree and hit the ground unharmed. Katie took a seat in the grass and leaned her back against the truck of the old oak tree, pulling her knees in to her chest.

Myra lowered herself to the ground and sat next to Katie, groaning slightly as she bent. Her knees were acting up again, though she'd hardly had any time to even notice.

"You know your father loves you very much," Myra began. "He's up there asking for you, Katie. He wants to see you."

Katie turned her face and looked off toward the foothills to the north. At the higher elevations, the leaves had already turned deep yellow and orange, and the hills looked like they were on fire.

"I know how hard this is for you," Myra said softly, brushing Katie's hair out of her face. "It's hard for us all to see him like this, but you're his daughter. I know you're in terrible pain. I don't know everything you're going through, but I can imagine."

Katie frowned. "This wasn't supposed to happen," she said, still looking away.

"I know it wasn't. None of this was. It's all just . . . like a horrible dream. And there's not much we can do but try to be there for each other as best we can."

"But he was better yesterday!" Katie insisted. "How could this happen again? How could he be riding his bike yesterday, and look totally normal, and then be stuck in bed again today? I thought it was just the flu! I thought he was going to get better!"

Myra sighed. "I know, I know. We were all so hopeful. We all wanted him to be better. But I guess sometimes people rebound a little as their body fights an illness, then it just comes back stronger than ever. And this radiation sickness – it's something I've never seen before. We were unprepared for it. We just didn't know what to expect."

"I hate this. I wish he'd never gone outside that day."

"I understand. All these years, he wanted to do right by you, and for the most part, he has. He's always been there for you. He's always been there for everyone."

Katie exhaled sharply. "That's what got him into this

mess in the first place. He was all worried about that little kid."

Myra nodded. "I understand you're angry at him. He made a mistake. He meant well, but it turned out to be a horrible mistake that he can't fix. And more than that – you're angry at the world right now. None of this is fair."

"It's not fair at all!" Katie snapped. "All of my friends have both their parents. I don't have a mother, and now . . ."

"I'm so sorry, Katie," Myra said tenderly. "You've been through so much. I wish I could make everything better for you."

Katie was silent for a moment, then she turned to look at her grandmother. Tears were brimming in her eyes. "He looked so . . . gray. He looked so sick, and weak. Like an old man. He didn't look like my dad. I – I just don't think I can see him like that."

Myra put her arm around Katie's shoulders and drew the girl in.

"If you don't go see him now, you'll regret it the rest of your life," Myra whispered. "Trust me on that. I know you think you know better than all the adults in your life, but I know that much. You have to go say goodbye."

For several moments, Katie let herself be held by her grandmother. The girl's red hair fell over her face, creating a shroud around her, and she closed her eyes.

Finally, she sat up, sniffed and pushed the curls away from her eyes. She looked up toward Brody's bedroom window, then at Myra.

"I'm ready."

Heather looked up to see Katie standing in the doorway. Myra stood behind her

"Look who I found," Myra said, squeezing Katie's shoulder.

Katie stood staring at her father in shock and disbelief. She cautiously took a few steps inside the room, coming to a stop at the foot of Brody's bed.

"Katie," Brody said as his eyes focused on his daughter. His voice was weak, but he worked to make it steady.

"Hi, Dad."

Heather wiped the tears from her face before Katie could see and stood up slowly. "I'm going to leave you two alone. Okay, Brody?"

"Okay," he said, and nodded at his sister.

Heather walked slowly through the room, giving Katie a half smile. "We'll just be downstairs," she said as she pulled the door closed behind her.

Brody smiled at his daughter. "Come sit down," he said in a raspy voice.

Katie moved to the chair beside the bed and sat down nervously.

"Dad, I'm sorry I didn't come up here sooner," Katie sputtered. "I just – I –"

Brody waved away her concern with a slight gesture of his hand. "It's okay. It's me who needs to apologize."

He took a slow, deep breath.

"I'm sorry I wasn't there for you when you needed me," he said slowly. "I should have stayed with you that day. And I'm so, so sorry I won't be there in the future."

"Dad, no," Katie protested, shaking her head furiously. "You're going to get better!"

Brody lifted his hand a bit from the bed to stop her. "Just let me tell you what I need to say."

Katie nodded and looked down at her hands.

"I know this is all scary. But you're going to be just fine," he said. "You're a very strong, smart girl. I know you can make it, even though the world is so different now."

Katie burst into tears and leaned across the bed, throwing her arms across his shoulders.

"No, Dad, no," she begged. "Please don't leave me!"

He embraced her, and for a moment remembered the time when she was little and hugs were more frequent. At that moment, as she clung to her father, she still looked like the same little girl.

"Shhh, it's going to be okay, Katie."

Her shoulders shook as she wept. He held her, though he could feel himself growing weaker. He could feel time running out.

"Listen to your grandmother, Katie. She's a good woman. Your aunt, too. Always try to do the right thing in life. And Katie, always remember that I love you."

His voice was barely above a whisper now. His hands grew weak, and fell down to his side. Speaking had used all his strength.

"I'm sorry," Katie said between sobs, pulling away to look at him. "I'm sorry I was mean to you. I don't know why I'm like that."

He smiled at her. "You have nothing to apologize for, my daughter."

He turned his head away to cough into the pillow, and she watched him through her tears. Letting his head collapse into the bed once more, he blinked and struggled to focus on her again. But he did, resting his vision on her sparkling, green eyes.

"You've made me so proud," he whispered.

34

Paul shielded the sun from his eyes with his hand. He was walking west on a small highway, halfway between Corsicana and Waco.

He had gotten an early start today after spending a restless night trying to fall asleep.

Luckily, he hadn't seen any more visions of his dead wife. But he still saw reminders of her and his children everywhere. The abandoned minivan on the side of the road like the one Marie drove, the porch swing like the one the kids had piled onto when they visited Marie's parents. Discarded candy wrappers, advertisements from a newspaper blowing down the road – everything in the world, it seemed, reminded Paul of what he had lost.

All he could do was keep walking. He moved fast, as if he could outrun the bits of memories that kept popping up around him. But wherever he went, his mind turned to his family.

He periodically asked himself mental questions as if to test his own sanity. What was his age, what was the date (or his best guess), what had been the events of the past week?

Of course, there was no objective third party to measure his responses, but he at least *thought* he was still mentally competent at the moment.

He didn't seem to be losing his mind.

But how could he know for sure?

And what if those visions of Marie came back? Or worse, what if he found himself in some strange place and he couldn't remember how he got there? The experience of waking up two days ago disoriented in the middle of the forest and not remembering how he had gotten there was one he didn't want to repeat.

So he tried to keep his mind sharp. He did mental arithmetic problems as he walked. He constantly calculated how many miles he had yet to cover, and how many he had put behind him. But because he didn't want to spiral down into a black hole again, he tried to avoid actively recalling memories of his wife and children – at least not yet.

Instead, he tried to remember parts of his childhood. He brought up every detail possible of growing up in the country – helping his dad on the farm, playing with Jack and the neighbor kids, listening to his parents laughing as they danced in the living room when they were in a good mood. There seemed to be a lot of love to go around back then. Paul wondered how things could have changed so much in his own lifetime.

Maybe part of him was hoping the return to Loretta would mean a return to those simpler days. He caught himself thinking that he would go back there and find it just as it always was, the small rural area that time seemed to pass by. But he knew that change had come to even small towns. And worst of all, the attacks had affected even the rural areas he walked through now.

His childhood home would not be the same. His parents

were gone. But maybe, just maybe, Jack would be there. Maybe there was something left of this life to go on fighting for.

And so he kept walking. And he would keep at it for a few more days until he arrived. He would make it to Loretta, one way or another. He didn't know what would be waiting for him there. He had to prepare himself for the worst. Everything would be different, changed.

Paul didn't fear for his own safety. He wasn't concerned with attacks from the criminal elements he knew were roaming free without check on the streets. What worried him was something darker, more ambiguous.

He just hoped that he could keep his own inner demons at bay.

35

Katie finally left her father's room and dragged herself down the hall, feeling like her legs were filled with lead. She came to a stop at the top of the stairs. Myra and Heather, who were waiting tensely downstairs in the living room, looked up at her expectantly.

"He wants to see you both," Katie said before turning back toward the room.

Myra and Heather followed Katie back into the room. The three of them kept vigil at Brody's side, each of them saying goodbye in their own way. Outside the window, the light began to fade as the day drew to a close.

KATIE WOKE the next morning in her own bed. She didn't remember when she had finally fallen asleep, but she had stayed at her father's side until the wee hours of the morning.

He had gone peacefully.

Brody didn't speak much after his time with Katie. He

just lay there in bed, resting his eyes at times, then looking at each of them in turn.

He, too, had said his goodbye.

After she woke up, Katie lay in her own bed for a long time, looking at the oak tree through the window.

She could hardly believe it had happened. She knew it was true, but even now, it seemed like a terrible dream. How was it possible? He had been healthy and strong just one week before. She had expected him to stay that way forever, or at least for the time being. At least long enough to see her grow up.

How could he be gone?

Katie's throat was sore and filled with a lump, but she didn't cry. She just felt a dull numbness. She didn't know if that would ever change. Nothing, she was sure, would ever return to normal.

Finally, Myra knocked at her door to check on her. Her grandmother walked in the room and wrapped Katie in a hug.

"I'm making lunch downstairs," she said.

In a numb sort of daze, Katie got dressed and went down to the living area. Heather and Myra, whose faces were tear-stained and tired looking, each gave her a hug, and then she joined her family at the dining room table. The three of them stared at the food on their plates, but no one ate. The three of them were in a daze, still reeling from watching Brody slip away.

"Brody was a good man," Myra said softly.

"One of the best," Heather said, not lifting her eyes.

After another long silence, Heather finally reached toward the plate of sandwiches in the middle of the table. She served herself some food, then began to pick at it.

"I'm going back out to look for Dad on the bike," Heather said. "Guess I should eat something."

"Heather, you've been out there looking for him all day," Myra said. "And you stayed up all night. You need rest. You're going to run yourself ragged."

Heather shrugged. "It doesn't matter. I have to *do* something. We just lost Brody. I don't want to lose Dad, too."

Myra shook her head and looked down at her lap. "I know."

"But you're just giving up on Dad, aren't you?" Heather asked. "Well, I'm not really to give up on him."

"I'm not giving up on him either, Heather," Myra said. "But you've gotten almost no sleep the past two nights. I just want you to take care of yourself."

Heather looked down at her plate and took a bite of her sandwich. She glanced out the window as she ate half-heartedly.

"I can help you look," Katie said in a hoarse voice.

Heather and Myra looked at her.

"Are you sure, Katie?" Myra asked. "It's fine if you don't feel up to it."

"No, I want to do it," Katie muttered. "I want to get out of the house."

Her eyes flicked up toward the stairs, then back to her plate.

Heather followed Katie's gaze toward the stairs, toward Brody's room. "We'll have to bury him. I was thinking about under the willow tree in the backyard. I can start digging this evening. It'll take me a while, though, to get it deep enough."

Myra gave her a slight frown. "Let's not talk about that right now."

Heather dropped her sandwich on the plate. "When do you want to talk about it?" she snapped.

Myra raised her hand to shush Heather, but Heather pushed her chair away from the table.

"And while we're discussing difficult topics, what are we going to do about firewood? Why is the woodshed empty?"

"Your father and I ordered three cords of wood last week," Myra said quietly. "It was going to be delivered tomorrow."

Heather exhaled sharply. "I guess that's not going to happen now. We need wood for heat. It's already starting to get cold." She began to pace back and forth across the living room. "And what about water?" Heather asked, glancing toward the supply of five-gallon water bottles. "That will last us two weeks if we're lucky. What then?"

Myra glanced at Katie. "Heather, can we talk about this later?"

"No, we can't," Heather said. "We can't keep skirting around all this. We've got to think about the future. We've got to make some decisions."

Myra sighed. "I *have* been thinking about it. I've been thinking about it all the time."

Heather snapped her head to look at her mother and stared at her with a pained expression on her face. "Then what are we going to do, Mom? How are we going to survive? We're in the middle of a national collapse, and we're not prepared at all."

"I don't have all the answers, sweetie. But for starters, the creek has water. We could bottle some and carry it home on the bikes. We'd boil it, of course. I'm sure that would help tide us over for a while."

"But for how long?" Heather asked. "And where will we get food? We can't just go to the store anymore. And I know you have a few veggies in the garden, but it's not enough to feed us all winter."

"You're right," Myra said. "I don't have a plan for how to survive here long-term. The simple fact is, we'll have to leave here eventually."

Heather stopped pacing and looked at her.

"Leave? Where will we go?"

"Texas," Myra said calmly. "It's the only place we *can* go."

Katie watched as Heather let the words sink in. "Do you mean to Austin, to be with Annie and Jack?" Heather asked.

Myra shook her head. "Yes, to be with Annie and Jack. But not Austin. That little town where Jack's from. Annie said something to me once, how they had planned to go to his childhood home if things in Austin ever got too bad."

Heather pondered that. "Yeah, I'm sure Austin is bad enough for them to leave, judging from what I've seen between here and Roanoke. It's probably worse in the big cities. But what about Dad? We're just going to leave him?"

Myra stood up and walked to the window, looking out on the front yard. "No, we won't leave him behind. We're going to keep searching for him. Every day. And tomorrow, we can go into town. I want to try to track down a few more people who might have seen him at the hardware store. Maybe they'll have some idea of what he was doing in the woods."

"That's a good idea," Heather conceded.

"We're going to find him, bring him back home," Myra said. "And then he'll go with us to Texas."

Heather crossed her arms over her shoulders and frowned. "Good. I'm glad you're not giving up on him."

Myra looked back at her. "Of course I'm not giving up. Your father wouldn't give up on us, would he?"

Heather shook her head. "No, he wouldn't." She bit her

lip and inhaled abruptly. "But . . . " she began and hesitated. "But what if we can't find him?"

Myra looked back at the window. "Then at some point we'll have to start thinking about leaving. I hope it never comes to this – believe me, I truly don't – but at some point, we will have to move on."

Heather collapsed into the recliner, her father's favorite. Her face crumpled in agony at the thought.

"We'll search those woods high and low," Myra said. "I promise. But the longer we go without finding him . . ."

Heather sniffed. "The less likely it is we'll ever find him."

Myra sat down near Heather on the couch. "I don't like this any more than you do," she said. "I love your father dearly, and the thought of leaving without him is unbearable. But I just don't think we can make it on our own here."

"How long should we wait before leaving?" Heather asked.

"I was thinking two weeks," Myra said. "Maybe a week or so more if we can get enough water."

"Okay," Heather said quietly. "I can live with that."

Katie stood up and moved toward the living room to join them. "We're not exactly invited, though, are we?" Katie asked. "You don't think they would mind us showing up there?"

"No, not at all," Myra said. "I know Annie too well. Jack too. They'd want us with them. Besides, there's safety in numbers. If the government doesn't help – if they don't get the vehicles and the electrical grid running again soon, we'll be on our own for who knows how long."

"That means no internet and no phones, right?" Katie asked.

"Right, and no food distribution, either," Myra said,

making room for Katie on the couch. "We'll all be sent back into the nineteenth century."

Heather snorted. "At least they had trains back then."

"The point is we'll all be on our own," Myra said. "We'll have to grow or raise any food we can't find. And it takes a lot of work to grow all your own food."

"What about the police or 911? The fire department?" Katie asked.

Myra shook her head. "We won't be able to rely on any of that, maybe not for a long time. So we'll have to look out for one another."

Katie glanced at the front door, then at the shotgun in the corner.

"Yes, we'll have to defend ourselves. We're too vulnerable, the three of us here on our own," Myra said.

"So we're going to Texas because it's dangerous here?" Katie asked.

"It's dangerous everywhere," Heather said. "The trip will be dangerous."

"It's not just safety," Myra said, "though that's part of it. It's easier to live in a community, for defense and for growing food. And yes, the trip will be dangerous. But we can do it."

"And it's because of Annie, too?" Heather asked. "You miss her?"

Myra smiled. "That's part of it."

"I miss her too. It would be nice to be closer to her and Jack now that everything's falling apart," Heather said, shaking her head. "But we haven't even talked about the hardest part! How on Earth will we get there? It's got to be around a thousand miles to the middle of Texas."

"We have bikes, don't we?" Myra asked.

"That'll take forever!" Heather said bitterly.

"You're forgetting your father and I hiked the entire Appalachian Trail," Myra said, her eyes twinkling.

"That was – what? – thirty years ago?" Heather asked. "Mom, listen. I rode a lot fewer miles then what it would take to get to Texas. And believe me, it's not pretty out there. And it's not easy, either. What about your knees?"

Myra bent down and reflexively rubbed at her knees. "I'll be okay. I can make it. I know it'll take a long time. But we have to try, don't we? We don't have enough food here to last more than a month, and the water will last us even less."

"Would Johnson City be on the way?" Katie asked.

"Yes, I think it would," Myra answered.

"We have a lot of beef jerky and trail mix back at the house," Katie said hopefully. "Dad and I couldn't bring it all. Maybe we could stop there and load up on the way."

Myra smiled at her granddaughter. "Excellent idea. That would be good traveling food."

Heather shook her head. "I don't know, Mom. We're talking about a huge journey here. Especially on bikes. Especially after all the attacks. Everything's falling apart out there."

Myra reached for Heather's hand. "I know. But we have to try, don't we?"

Myra looked over at Katie and grabbed her hand as well. "What do you think, Katie?"

Katie glanced at Heather, then back at Myra. "Maybe it would be best. It does feel a little scary out here in the middle of nowhere. And I mean, we'll hopefully find Grandpa first, right?"

"Yes, of course," Myra said. She looked at her daughter.

"Okay, I can agree to it," Heather said. "It's crazy, but the whole world is crazy now, and we have to survive somehow.

We don't have enough food, firewood, or a water source here. I don't know how we can make it work."

"We're going to survive," Myra said. "Whatever we decide to do. We'll find a way to make it through this. And not just physically. We'll find a way to live through the heartbreak, too."

She looked at Katie and gave her a knowing look. The teen nodded, even as she felt a lump in her throat.

Heather stood up and tore into her sandwich, suddenly hungry. "But I'm going to spend the time searching for Dad. Every day."

Myra nodded. "I'll go out with you," she said as she returned to the table and took a bite of a peanut butter-and-honey sandwich. "We can cover a lot of ground before dark if we leave soon."

Katie watched them from her place on the sofa for a moment, feeling an emptiness in her chest. But somewhere down deep, there was a tiny spark of hope as well.

Her father was gone. She knew she would never recover from the terrible loss.

But somehow, she knew she would go on living. She wasn't all alone. With what was left of her family, she was going to survive.

36

"Annie, quit fussing over me! I'll be fine!"

From her place on the living room sofa, Charlotte waved Annie off.

"Okay, okay," Annie said, raising her hands. "I just want to make sure you have everything you need."

"I'm fine," Charlotte promised. "You changed my dressings, you fed me. I have plenty of blankets. I think I'm good for the night."

Annie picked the paper plates off the coffee table and carried them to the darkened kitchen. Their second day in the ranch house was coming to an end, and she was gearing down for another night in the house. The bed with clean linens had been comfortable last night, and she had finally gotten a solid night's sleep, but she was still weary. The place just wasn't the same without Jack around.

She had spent the day cleaning and organizing the big, empty house. Now, the kitchen was filled with boxes and packages of food she had dragged out from the pantries and cabinets in order to inventory it all. But it had gotten dark before she could finish putting it all away. Now the disorder dragged her spirits down even more.

Tomorrow, she told herself. She'd get it all put away tomorrow.

She remembered when she and Jack had begun to stock food and water for the ranch house. It had been at least two or three years ago. It had been Jack's idea, and Annie was now grateful for his foresight. Along with the medical supplies and other essentials they had stored in the house, the food and water stores would keep her and Charlotte alive for a few months. It had been a lot of work to do all the planning, not to mention the constant rotation of supplies, but it had all been well worth it. Without all the work they had put into it, Annie and Charlotte's future would look very dim.

Annie was about to put the paper plates into the trash, but she stopped. There would have to be a radical change in the way she did things. No more garbage trucks picking up trash, and no more food delivery to the stores, meant there could be no more waste. The paper plates were basically clean – they could be used again. And she would have to start a compost pile. Any food scraps would be composted and broken down to enrich the soil and help them grow vegetables. Any inorganic waste would have to be burned, if possible.

She'd have to reclaim the old garden that had been abandoned years ago. It was covered in weeds, but at least the soil was still fertile and free of rocks, or so she hoped. In one of the cabinets in the house, she and Jack had ferreted away a variety of seeds. Maybe she could even plant a winter garden if she hurried.

She dragged herself back to the living room and blew

out one of the candles that were burning on the coffee table. They would have to conserve candles, too.

"We have to start waking up at dawn," Annie said, breathing a deep sigh. "And we'll have to go to bed soon after sundown. We don't have enough candles to stay up late."

"Sounds good," Charlotte agreed. She noticed the strain on Annie's face even in the dim candlelight. "Are you okay?"

Annie sank in the chair near the front window and leaned back. "I'm exhausted."

"I'll bet you are," Charlotte said. "You've been on your feet all day, getting this house in order. Not to mention your obsession over my wounds."

Outside, the wind picked up the screen door, which Annie had forgotten to latch, and slammed it shut. The sudden noise made Annie jump out of her chair and reach for the pistol. She soon realized it was just the wind, and she sighed and crossed to the door.

"Plus you're constantly on alert for bad guys," Charlotte said. "That would exhaust anyone."

Annie latched the screen door and returned to her seat. "There's just so much work to be done around here. Tomorrow I've got to finish the food inventory, and then I need to start work on the garden."

Charlotte gave her a sympathetic look. "I'm sorry I'm not more help. I'm just a big lug, stuck here on this couch."

"No, it's okay," Annie said. "It's not your fault, anyway. You were shot, for crying out loud. I need you to heal as much as possible. And besides, it's not just the work."

"You miss Jack."

Annie nodded. "I know it's unrealistic to think he would have made it here already, but I don't know. It's hard to keep the faith that he'll make it here."

"But you have to, Annie," Charlotte said. "You can't give up on him."

"I'm not giving up on him. I'm not giving up on him at all. It's just – I'm giving up on the world. I guess I don't trust anything anymore. I used to have a feeling that everything would work out in the end. I don't believe that anymore."

"But there's always hope. If you don't hold on to the hope that he'll return, it's going to be a lot harder to get through the day."

Annie nodded. "That's true. I do have hope he'll make it here, but sometimes hope is what hurts the most."

Charlotte frowned. "What do you mean?"

"It's just been one struggle after another since the attacks. One disappointment after the next. If Jack doesn't come back –"

Annie stopped abruptly. Her voice was shaking. She wiped away tears.

"I don't know how I'll be able to live with that disappointment. And it's more than disappointment. That's not the right word. More like, devastation."

Charlotte didn't say anything. She reached across the dark room and took Annie's hand in her own. She didn't make a noise from the pain from her wounds flaring, but Annie saw it on her face. Somehow, that gesture meant more to Annie than any words could.

"Thanks," Annie said, squeezing Charlotte's hand.

"He'll be back," Charlotte said.

Annie nodded and let go of her hand. She pushed herself to her feet and blew out the remaining candle.

"Let's try to get some rest," Annie said.

Charlotte settled into her makeshift bed, pulling the covers up under her chin. "Sleep well," she said.

"You too," Annie said as she began to climb the stairs. "See you in the morning."

Inside her bedroom, Annie closed the door behind her and crawled into bed without changing her clothes. She was ready for the day to be over. She got under the covers and curled into a ball. Tomorrow would be another big day, and she needed her rest.

Everything was riding on her labor. If she slacked off, it wasn't a matter of picking up the loose ends the next day. An off day or two could make the difference between surviving or not.

Despite her fatigue, she didn't drift off right away. Her mind roiled with worries. But gradually, the weariness took her over, and her thoughts began to fall away.

A flash of light woke her from her half-asleep state. Her eyes flew open and she threw the blanket off her body. Her heart racing, she leapt from the bed and ran to the window.

Someone was outside.

37

A vehicle on the highway slowed and turned in the driveway.

Someone was coming to the house.

Without stopping to think, Annie grabbed the pistol and ran downstairs. The sound of her footsteps woke Charlotte.

"What is it?" Charlotte asked groggily.

"*Shhh*. Keep quiet. Someone just pulled into the driveway," Annie whispered as she moved to the front window. She pulled the curtain back just a bit and peered outside, keeping her body hidden behind the wall.

Behind her, Charlotte struggled to her feet and grabbed the chef's knife she kept within reach on the coffee table.

Annie's hand trembled as she clenched the pistol. The vehicle made its way to the top of the driveway and parked at the edge of the front yard.

Why was someone pulling into the driveway at this hour? What did they want?

The wave of fear coursed higher through Annie's chest as she realized that it was indeed *they*. She made out three figures in the vehicle as the driver killed the engine.

Annie looked desperately over at Charlotte, who watched from the side window.

"He's got a gun," Charlotte whispered frantically.

Annie looked back at the vehicle. The driver was holding a rifle as he jumped from the vehicle. The sound of his slamming door made her jump.

Please let them go away.

Annie took a deep breath. She would have to do something. She didn't know if she could defend the house against three people, one with a big rifle, but she would have to try.

She looked around, trying to figure out what to do with herself. Should she start shooting from the window now? Should she wait until they tried to break in? She swallowed as bile rose in her throat.

Outside, the driver took a few steps forward. Gravel crunched beneath his boots. Finally, he spoke.

"Annie?"

Jack!

Annie threw the front door open and stood staring in the doorway with her mouth open.

Was it him, or was her mind playing tricks on her? Could it really be him, finally?

"Annie! Oh, God, it's you!" his familiar voice came.

Annie tried to push the screen door open, forgetting it had been latched, and fumbling with it in frustration. Finally, she emerged from the house just as he set his rifle down and ran up the porch.

"Jack! It's you!"

He bounded the steps and then, just like that, he was standing before her. Her eyes moved over his face quickly, still in shock and confusion, and then he took her in his arms.

She felt her shoulders shake from a mix of laughter and tears as she held him close.

"You finally made it back to me," she said, murmuring into his chest.

He pulled back to look at her, studying her face in the darkness.

"I was so afraid this house would be empty," he said, trailing the back of his hand down her cheek. "I was so afraid I'd lost you."

She nodded, tears falling from her eyes. "I was so afraid I'd lost *you*."

She looked over the bruises and cuts on his face, the long stubble marking the passage of time, the way he held his body – he was clearly in pain from various injuries.

He had been through so much – they *both* had. The weight of it all hit her all at once. They had come so close to losing each other. She buried her face against his jacket once more, and he held her tight.

The sound of movement behind her startled her.

"It's about time you showed up."

Jack looked up to see Charlotte standing behind them on the porch, leaning against the doorway with a big grin on her face.

"Charlotte?" he asked. "Is that you?"

"In the flesh."

Jack returned the smile, happy to see another familiar face, and glad that his wife hadn't been alone all this time. He turned to look at the Porsche. "Whose car is that?"

Annie looked back at Charlotte. "Long story," Annie said, her eyes sparkling. "But how did you make it all the way from LA?" she asked. "Whose truck is that?"

Jack turned to the Bronco to see Brent and Naomi getting out of the vehicle.

"I guess we all have some catching up to do," Jack said. "But first, introductions."

38

"More reconstituted mashed potatoes, Naomi?" Annie asked as she passed the serving bowl around the table. "They at least *remind* you of homemade."

Naomi laughed and took the bowl from Annie. Jack looked down at his own plate as he finished up his first serving, then took seconds of everything. It was the first decent meal he'd had in a week, and he was ravenous.

Across the table, Brent and Charlotte were laughing about the antics of some minor Austin celebrities. The two had never before met, but they had hit it off in a friendly kind of way.

The five of them had slept in – rising with the sun would begin tomorrow, they agreed – and were now enjoying lunch prepared over the gas stove from an assortment of items from the pantry.

Jack watched as Annie exchanged some pleasantries with Naomi. Jack had told his wife about Naomi's story, and how she had reluctantly accepted his help. Annie was happy to help out the young woman, especially after all Naomi had been through.

As for Brent, Annie had met him a few times before at Jack's office parties. He seemed a bit more mature this time around, which was good. Maybe surviving the attacks had made them *all* wise up a little.

Jack had been a little nervous to bring two new people to the house, but Annie was so far pleased. The ranch house was a little isolated, it was true, especially since most of the neighbors Jack had grown up with had moved away over the years. The extra company not only made the house less lonely, but the extra hands would be welcome as they set about making the homestead self-sustainable.

Naomi, for her part, seemed unsure of her new surroundings, but open to the change. In any case, the despondency that had taken root on her face seemed to be lightening. She knew that LA was no longer a place she could survive in, and she was grateful to the Hawthornes for giving her a new home.

After lunch, Jack and Annie excused themselves for a walk around the property. They left Naomi and Brent in charge of clean-up, and Charlotte returned to the living room to rest.

"Thanks for taking care of my wife while I was gone," Jack said to Charlotte as he walked past the couch and headed toward the front door.

Charlotte laughed. "More like she took care of me!"

Jack smiled. He had already heard the stories, and his comment was tongue-in-cheek.

"Really, Jack, you should see her with that gun!" Charlotte said, grinning at Annie. "She's a modern day Annie Oakley. I wouldn't get on her bad side if I were you."

Jack winked at his wife. "I won't."

Outside, Jack and Annie stepped out on the porch. Jack turned to look at her, and she gave him a smile.

It was that smile he had missed so much. He still could hardly believe he was back home.

"I thought you didn't hear me on the phone that day," he said. "I thought I'd have to go all the way to Austin to find you."

"Wait, when? What did you think I didn't hear?" Annie asked, frowning.

Jack looked at her. "Just before we lost the connection. I told you to get out of Austin, to come here."

Annie shook her head. "No, I never heard you. But it didn't take long to figure out that the city was too dangerous. This was the best option we had. Especially when our house was taken over by squatters."

Jack felt a rush of anxiety as he recalled Annie's stories of her encounters. All the near misses. He had come so close to never seeing her again.

The anxiety was quickly replaced by elation as it hit him just how lucky he had been. He scooped her up around her waist and carried her playfully down the stairs as she yelped and laughed in his ear. He returned her to her feet on a clump of grass near the front step.

The two walked hand-in-hand toward the backyard. She talked excitedly to him about her ideas for the garden. He did his best to listen, but he often found his thoughts drifting to the horrors he had seen in White Rock.

Last night, Jack had told Annie the summary about what had happened there, but he hadn't gone over every gory detail. She had listened with wide eyes, shocked by what he had seen in Arizona.

Today, he walked with a rifle slung over his shoulder. He

didn't know if he'd ever be able to let his guard down again. And he figured that was a good thing.

"With five of us, our food supply won't last through the winter," Annie said. "I'm hoping I can get some potatoes and cabbage going."

Jack nodded. "We might have to go out and do some scavenging in abandoned houses or stores. We'll need more food sooner or later. It's better to stock up now. And I want to fill the gas tanks up, maybe find some more warm clothes. Odds and ends."

Annie turned to look at him with fear in her eyes. "I hate the idea of going back out there. It's so dangerous." She sighed. "But I know you're right. We don't have enough here."

They stood before the old garden patch, which was overrun with hearty weeds.

"Getting this garden in shape is going to take some work," Annie said. "Oh, and some animal protein would be good. Maybe someone in town would trade us a couple of chickens for some packaged food. Eventually, we'll need more animals if the power doesn't come back on anytime soon. And goats, too. But well, the garden and maybe some eggs would be a good start."

"Good idea," Jack said. "And we'll have to do some repairs to the house. The roof looks bad in a few places. But first things first – we'll need some kind of outhouse. Maybe a composting toilet."

Annie nodded. "Yeah, definitely."

"And this garden won't be big enough," Jack said, staring at the patch he used to work in as a teenager. "We'll have to expand it by quite a bit."

Annie nodded. "I can start today. Brent and Naomi can help us, right?"

Jack smiled. "Yeah, I think they both have experience digging."

Annie bent and pulled at some weeds. "This native grass is tough. Strong root system."

Jack nodded. "I know those weeds well." He walked along the edge of the garden, where he and his brother had spent so many hours weeding and watering. Now that he was back in his old childhood home, his thoughts often turned to Paul. Jack wished they had sorted things out between them years ago. Now, there was no way to contact his brother. Wherever he was, Jack hoped he was well.

And Jack knew that Annie was thinking about her own family. Her parents lived in an isolated spot, and her brother, sister and niece were scattered throughout their pockets of the southeast. Jack could sense Annie's growing worry over her family, and her desire to see them again.

As Annie inspected the soil, Jack looked over the property, his eyes drifting out to the empty highway. The five of them had a lot of work ahead. They weren't in the lap of luxury by any means, but they had a lot more than many people, especially after the attacks. And their relative advantage meant that they would be a target.

Out there in the country, several miles away from even a tiny town, and sitting on several valuable resources – they were vulnerable. They'd have to be vigilant to protect their food, water, weapons, and home.

Somehow, Jack knew the fight wasn't over. He'd have to go on protecting what he cared about, and fighting to ensure they could go on living.

"Jack? You okay?"

Annie looked over at him from her corner of the garden, then began to cross the distance toward him. He met her halfway and wrapped an arm around her shoulders.

"Fine," he said, smiling and pulling her close.

"You look lost in thought," she said, smiling at him.

"I was just thinking about what it took for us all to get here," he said. "How hard it was to get to this place right here."

Annie nodded. "We did the impossible – we found each other. And we made it out here."

"If we can do that, we can do anything," Jack said, smiling at his wife. "As long as we're together, we're going to make it."

Thank you for reading Survive the End, Book 3 in the Atomic Threat series.

If you enjoyed this book, I'd really appreciate it if you could review it on Amazon. The book market can be tough, and every little review helps!

Be sure to sign up for my spam-free newsletter here so you won't miss any new releases:

http://eepurl.com/c5xziP

Until next time,
    Dave

ABOUT THE AUTHOR

Dave Bowman is a writer and native Texan. When he's not writing about the end of the world as we know it, he can be found planning for his future homestead or haunting his favorite barbecue joint.

ALSO BY DAVE BOWMAN

Read my other post-apocalyptic thrillers:

Survive the Blast (Atomic Threat, Book 1)
Get Out Alive (Atomic Threat, Book 2)

Fight to Survive (After the Outbreak, Book 1)
Fight to Live (After the Outbreak, Book 2)
Fight to Be Free (After the Outbreak, Book 3)

Sign up to my spam-free mailing list and never miss a new release:

http://eepurl.com/c5xziP

Made in United States
Orlando, FL
01 December 2024